M000195895

THE FORGOTTEN PACT

IONA ROSE

AUTHOR'S NOTE

Hey there!

Thank you for choosing my book. I sure hope that you love it. I'd hate to part ways once you're done though. So how about we stay in touch?

My newsletter is a great way to discover more about me and my books. Where you'll find frequent exclusive give-aways, sneak previews of new releases and be first to see new cover reveals.

And as a HUGE thank you for joining, you'll receive a FREE book on me!

With love,

Iona

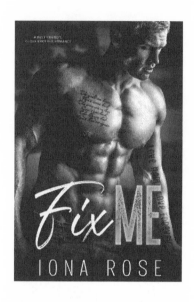

Get Your FREE Book Here:
https://dl.bookfunnel.com/v9yit8b3f7

Publisher: Some Books

978-1-913990-53-4

1

CLARISSA

I can't help but smile as I get off the bus at the bus station and look around. I wasn't sure how I would feel coming back here after all of these years, but with the familiar scent of jasmine in the air welcoming me home, I'm so glad I'm here. It's like stepping back in time, back into my childhood. All at once, I feel a rush of nostalgia go through me. I feel as though it's been forever since I was here and yet at the same time, I feel as though I've never been away from the place.

I leave the bus stop and start walking through the town. The apartment I've rented isn't far from the bus stop and it's a nice enough day. I was all set to take a cab to my apartment building, but I find that I want to walk, to soak up the atmosphere of the town and reminisce somewhat. Most of my things have already been sent to my apartment with the moving company and I only have a weekend bag with me so it's not like I'm laden down with luggage.

It's been fourteen years since my dad got offered a job in Italy. I was fifteen and of course I hated the idea of moving away, but as a child, I didn't get a say in the matter and before I knew it, I was in Rome. Rome is a beautiful place and looking back now, I'm glad we went. It will always hold a special place in my heart, but it's no St. Augustine. This feels like coming home in a way that returning to Rome after college just didn't.

I smile to myself as I pass the park we used to play in when we were kids. We would spend hours there in the summer and on weekends and evenings after school.

Nothing much has changed in the park. I can see the swing set, the top of the slide, the duck pond and the bandstand. The trees are taller, and the flower beds are different, but aside from that, it almost feels like I've gone back in time rather than just come back to town. I suppose that's part of the appeal of a small town like St. Augustine – nothing changes, meaning people will always feel at home here, even if that hasn't technically been true for almost a decade and a half.

I round the corner at the edge of the park and my smile widens when I see the large oak tree with our tire swing still attached to it. The tree has grown a lot over the years and the tire swing is now too high for any kids to be able to play on it, but the fact it's still there is amazing to me.

The tire swing reminds me of long, hot summer days when Gabe, my best friend at the time, and I would come down here and spend all day on that swing, daring each other to go higher and higher. I miss those days and I miss Gabe. We were inseparable for years before I was whisked off to Italy. We made the odd call to each other after my family and I moved away but long-distance calls are so expensive and both of our parents used to moan at us about the phone bills and eventually, we just lost touch.

I hope he's still here somewhere in town, so I get to see him again. It's been so long, and we would have so much to catch up on. He could no doubt tell me about his successful career, his beautiful wife and adorable children. And in turn, I could tell him about my failed career and my cheating ex-boyfriend.

I wonder if he remembers that night in the bandstand. The night we... I smile and shake away the memory. I really don't need to go back there. He probably won't remember it and even if he does, so what? It's not like it's actually going to happen.

I realize I've walked the rest of the way to my new apartment building without really noticing anything more around me while I was lost in thought. I feel a surge of excitement go through me as I open the main door and head for the elevator. For all of the things here that are so familiar to me, this is still a fresh start for me, and I can't wait to start on my new life and leave the old one – the one where I get cheated on and get my heart broken – very firmly behind me.

I step out of the elevator on the ninth floor and walk down the hallway. It's a nice hallway, carpeted in dark blue. The carpet is clean as are the cream-colored walls and the pleasant smells I catch in the air as they drift out of people's apartments, food cooking, laundry detergent, something sweet and fruity that may or may not be a candle burning. It's definitely an improvement on the apartments in my last place.

When Michael cheated on me, I felt as though my world had ended. I thought we were in love, but I was wrong. I was in love. Michael claimed to be in love with me but the fact that he would fuck some skanky little secretary from the office told me otherwise. Despite loving Michael, I still had enough self-respect that there was no way I was staying in a relationship with him after that. The place we were living in was his and I moved out the very day I found out about his affair.

I remember walking the streets with a suitcase containing my clothes and my makeup and my toiletries – the only things that were actually mine. Everything else in the apartment was Michael's – I had given up all my furniture, everything I owned really when I moved in with him. As I walked, I tried to work out what the hell I was supposed to do next.

The rain started then and within minutes, I was soaked through to the skin. I was shivering in the cold with my hair sticking to my scalp, the rain mixing with my tears and streaking my makeup. I checked into a hotel for the night. It was all I could think of to do at that time. I didn't want to turn up at a friend's place looking so disheveled.

The next morning, I extended my stay while I worked out where I was going to go and what I was going to do. The first thing I did was call my boss and tell him I quit. I couldn't face going back to the office after what Michael had done. I knew I was the victim, and he was the one who should feel ashamed, but knowing that didn't change the way I felt. I couldn't stand the thought of going back to work and having them all laughing at me behind my back and talking about me. I would be the one they pitied. The one who couldn't keep her man satisfied. No thank you. I had more than enough to worry about without bringing that onto myself.

I began searching for another job pretty much instantly but word travels quickly through the finance sector and my boss had no qualms about telling other firms that I had left him in the lurch and refused to work my notice period. Naturally he didn't bother to tell them why. No finance company would touch me after that. And because of the way I left my job, I didn't get a PTO payout and staying at the hotel was eating my money like there was no tomorrow.

I had enough left for a deposit and a month's rent on a decent apartment and then I would be out of money. I began looking for both an apartment and a job outside of my comfort zone. I found both, neither of which exactly filled me with joy. I found a job waiting tables – something I really didn't enjoy in the least. After a few weeks there though, an opportunity opened up to work behind the bar instead. I took the opportunity and I loved it. My job situation felt much better, but my home life was still in shambles.

I had massively underestimated the cost of rent in the city and the only apartment that I could afford was a tiny thing. The living room also functioned as a dining room and a bedroom and it had a little kitchenette at the end, which meant that every time I cooked on the small stove, I risked setting my bedding on fire – that's how small the room was. The bathroom was so small that if I gained so much as a pound, I didn't think I'd fit in my shower, and it wasn't like I was overweight to begin with.

My apartment's size was the least of my worries there though. My neighbors posed a bigger problem. The hallway leading to my apartment was covered in graffiti and smears of what could have been blood or feces – I didn't know which and I didn't want to know. It smelled of stale urine and boiled vegetables left to rot. The smells drifting from the other apartments told me that my neighbors were stoners or worse.

Six months I put up with that before I finally knew I'd had as much of the place as I could take. I had never felt as low as I did the night my circumstances really hit me. I opened a bottle of wine and that was my first mistake. The second bottle was my second mistake, but by far my biggest mistake was when I called Michael. In my drunken state, I had decided to call him and really make him understand what he had done to me when he betrayed me. I wanted him to feel my pain. Somehow though, I ended up in tears telling him how my life had gone so wrong lately and before I knew it, he was at my door. From there, it didn't take much before he was in my bed.

2

CLARISSA

The next morning, I felt regret like I had never felt before. My head was banging, I felt nauseous and worse than that, I felt ashamed of myself. Was I really so low that throwing myself at Michael had been an option?

I knew then I had to get away from the city, away from my shit hole apartment, away from my dead-end job and most importantly, away from Michael. And that's when I made the decision to come back to St. Augustine. For the same monthly rent, I have an apartment in a nice block that seems to house nice, normal people who don't smear shit up the walls and smoke drugs.

I fish my key back out of my purse and unlock the door to apartment thirty-six. I take a deep breath, steeling myself for whatever might lay inside. I've only seen the apartment in the realtor's photos and of course they are trained to make anything look good. I close my eyes, push the door open and step inside. I open my eyes and relief floods me.

I'm standing in a short hallway with four doors leading off it. So far so good. Doors mean rooms, separate rooms for separate things. I poke my head in the first one and find a bathroom. It's small but nowhere near as small as my old one. The shower is over a bath rather than in a cubicle and I imagine myself having long, lazy bubble baths with music playing, surrounded by candles and I smile at the image.

Buoyed up by the decent bathroom, I move on, feeling more confident that the place is going to be ok. I open the door opposite the bathroom and find myself in a large, open plan room. Again, it's an arrangement of the living room, dining room and kitchen but it is so much better than what I'm used to.

The kitchen is a full-sized kitchen with a breakfast bar with tall stools sectioning it off from the rest of the room. The dining area is equipped with a small wooden table and two chairs, and the living area has a large beige couch, a coffee table, two recliners and a TV on the wall. There's plenty of room, or at least there will be when I get around to unpacking all the boxes the movers have unceremoniously dumped in the middle of the living room.

I can't stop myself from smiling as I back out of the living room and view the other two doors. I open the one next to the living room and find a good-sized linen closet with shelves. I'm pleased about that as I never seem to have enough storage space. Finally, I open the door at the end of the hallway. I find a good-sized bedroom with a double bed, a wardrobe and a small cabinet beside the bed. I go right into the room and move over to the window, smiling to myself when I look out and see that I can see the park from here.

I spend the rest of the day unpacking my weekend bag and my boxes and by the time I flop down on the couch with a pizza, I feel like I've had a productive day. All my things are unpacked and put away and already the apartment is beginning to feel like home. I just know I'll be happy here.

As I eat my dinner, I think about what I'm going to do for work. I don't have any savings – getting this place took the last money I had. I know I could go back to my old job working as a personal assistant in the finance sector. After all, I haven't worked in the area for a while now, I have kept up with the changing trends, and I can't see my old boss feeling the need to try to sabotage me all the way over here. I just won't put his name on my resume.

At the minute though, I need an income and I need it fast. I don't want to rush into a bad job in a place I'm less than happy because I want this to work in the long term. I don't want to end up taking something I'm not happy with just because I have bills to pay. I decide that for now, I'm going to try and find a bar job to tide me over while I do some research on local finance companies and see what the sector has to offer in and around St. Augustine.

I finish my dinner and think for a moment. I go through to the bathroom and brush my teeth and then my short black hair. I use the toilet and then I leave the bathroom and grab my jacket and my purse. I head out of the apartment, locking the door behind me. There really is no better time to go looking for bar work than now – that time when the night-time drinkers are starting to come out and the pub is busy enough that the manager isn't trying to do paperwork undisturbed but not so busy that taking the chance to ask about an opportunity might be a nuisance.

It's a fairly nice night and I set off walking towards the main street. It's only a ten-minute walk but it takes me slightly longer than that as I go into two bars on the way. Both of them are deathly quiet and unsurprisingly, neither of them is currently looking for any new staff. I make my way onto the main street. This is the one part of the town that has changed considerably.

The shops I remember from my childhood are mostly gone, replaced with boutique clothing stores, convenience stores and a cute looking little thrift shop that I make a note to come back to when it's open. I vaguely remember my father drinking around here, a place called Landers or something like that. The spot where I remembered it being is now an Indian restaurant. There are still several bars along the street though, so I don't let myself get disheartened just yet.

I feel a smile creep over my face when I see a help wanted sign in the window of the next bar I come to. I stand back slightly and look up at the sign above the door. The sign tells me that the bar is called The Marlow Bar and Grill. It looks fairly small but respectable and I pull the door open and step inside.

The place is lit by dim hanging lights and candles. The atmosphere is intimate and cozy, the tables far enough apart to give the diners some privacy. The smell of grilling meat in the air makes my stomach rumble despite the fact I've just eaten. The hostess smiles at me from behind her lectern as I approach her.

"Hi. Welcome to The Marlow Bar and Grill. Do you have a reservation with us this evening?" she asks.

"No. I'm actually interested in the job you have advertised in the window for bar staff," I say.

"The position is actually to join the team of wait staff. If you're still interested I can grab the manager for you?" she says.

I think for a moment. Am I interested? I think back to my old job waitressing. The burnt arms. The drunken gropes. The yelling and complaining about things that weren't even my fault half of the time. The tables that stiffed me on tips and left me with a choice between heating and food. The people who barked their drink orders at me rather than returning my polite hello. No. I'm not interested. I can't go back to that. I smile and shake my head.

"No thank you," I say. "But can I leave my contact details in case a bar job opens up?"

"Of course," the hostess says.

She hands me a pen and a piece of paper. Her smile has never slipped the whole time we spoke, and she still smiles as I scribble down my details and hand her back the paper and the pen.

"Thanks," I say, although something tells me that as soon as I leave she will throw away the piece of paper I hand back to her.

Turning around I leave and continue my wandering. The next two places I try aren't hiring and I'm starting to get massively deflated. I keep walking though, interested to see what else has changed on the main street. I pass a bar and debate going inside but I decide against it. I'll try again tomorrow. I can only take so much rejection in one night.

I pass an opening that I think is a side street. I peer down it to see if it's home to any more shops and see it's no more than an alley really, but I work out that if I walk down it, I'll cut my walk home in half. I start to head into the alley when the building on the other side of it catches my eye. It's another pub and I can't help but smile when I see the name of the place, The Black Swan. When we were kids, Gabe always said he would buy a bar and call it The Black Swan. Could it possibly be his bar? Has he actually followed through on his dream?

I don't suppose it's going to be his bar. Chances are he's not even in town anymore. Still though, I am curious. If it is his bar, it would be great to see a friendly face and catch up with him. Maybe he has a wife now. Children too. It would be great to have a ready-made little family to befriend.

I push the door open. The bar is fairly busy but it's not rowdy yet and I can hear the jukebox playing over the sound of the chatter coming from the tables. I hear the clink of balls as a group huddle around a pool table. A cheer goes up as one of the players sinks the black ball and wins the game. I find myself smiling as the winner does a little victory dance around the table.

I head for the bar, already liking the friendly atmosphere here. As I reach the bar, I open my mouth to ask if Gabe is by any chance the manager here when the sign behind the bartender's head catches my eye: bar staff wanted.

"Hi," I say when the bartender comes towards me. "I'd like to apply for the job."

I nod towards the sign and the bartender smiles at me.

"Great," he says. He turns away from me. "Penny. You're needed up here." He turns back to me. "Penny's in charge. She will have a chat with you."

"Thanks," I say with a smile.

So, it's Penny's bar not Gabe's bar. Oh well. I never truly believed it would be his. But still, the coincidence makes me think it might be a sign that this is the bar I was meant to find a job in.

A short, red-haired woman appears through a door behind the bar. The bartender nods towards me and she walks across the bar area. She lifts the divider between the bar and the public area and steps around to me. She smiles widely and offers her hand. I take it and we shake hands.

"Hi. I'm Penny. You're interested in the bartender position?" she asks.

"Clarissa Blayde. And yes, I'm very much interested," I say, returning Penny's smile.

"Have you got ten minutes to have a quick chat?" Penny asks.

"Like an interview?" I ask. I look down at my jeans and shake my head. "I'm not dressed for an interview."

"Well, the fact you recognize that gives you brownie points," Penny says. "And I won't judge you for not dressing for something you didn't know was going to happen."

"Then I'm free to chat," I say.

Penny leads me to a small table away from the bar in a quieter area of the room. We sit down and she smiles again.

"Do you have any bartending experience?" she asks me.

"Yes," I reply, telling her about my old job and how I moved from waiting tables to bartending and loved it. She listens intently and then she nods her head.

"Ok Clarissa, I'm going to level with you here. I am seriously short-staffed right now and I need someone who can hit the ground running. You will obviously be shown how to work the cash register and that kind of thing, but I will expect you to work on your own initiative quickly. Is that something you feel comfortable with?" Penny asks.

That's the moment I know I have the job, but I don't want to come across as too cocky, so I resist the urge to smile. Instead, I nod.

"Of course. In my old bar job, I was often the only bartender working and many nights I was the last person to leave, meaning I was responsible for securing the premises," I say. And then I play my ace. "And having just moved here today, I don't have anywhere I need to give notice so I can start whenever you need me to."

"So, you're saying you could start tomorrow evening?" Penny asks.

"Sure," I say, nodding my head.

"Then you're hired," Penny says.

"Thank you," I say.

"Bring your paperwork and everything along tomorrow. Around six thirty so I can go through your paperwork and then give you a quick tour and you can start your shift at seven. Rebecca will be working with you, she'll show you the ropes and help you out if you have any questions or anything," Penny says. "There's no specific uniform but we ask all staff members to wear black. Whether that's pants or a skirt with a top or a dress is up to you."

"Ok," I say.

It all sounds pretty standard, and I am excited to start working. Suddenly I don't want to leave the warm, happy atmosphere of the bar and go back to my empty apartment and I'm trying to work out whether it would be appropriate for me to stay after this and have a drink when I realize that a shadow has fallen over the table and Penny is talking to me and gesturing towards the shadow. I've already missed the first part of what she said.

"...this is Gabe Kerrey. He owns the bar," Penny finishes.

3

CLARISSA

I look up, knowing the shock is clear to see on my face. I find myself looking into the eyes of Gabe. My old best friend Gabe. I'm not surprised by the rush of warmth I feel when I see him. I am surprised by the rush of wetness I feel in my pussy though as my muscles clench deliciously at the sight of him.

Gabe has changed more than anything else in St. Augustine. He has gotten smoking hot. Gone is the scrawny kid with the broken, old-fashioned glasses. Before me stands a man solid with muscles, the kind of sculpted body I just want to run my hands all over. His broken, old-fashioned glasses are gone, replaced by trendy black framed ones. His eyes haven't changed. Their brown depths still hold warmth and a sparkle of joy and playfulness.

And when he smiles, it's like going back in time. The way his lip curls up at the side, something I always noticed but didn't really pay any attention to, now is something that makes me shift in my seat as my clit tingles.

I swallow hard, aware that I've been staring at Gabe for

far too long. But he stares back at me, and I can't bring myself to look away from him in case it isn't real, and he vanishes again if I do. The seconds stretch into what feels like minutes although it can't really be that long. Penny clears her throat, sounding uncomfortable and that breaks the spell. Gabe looks away and I can finally move my eyes again.

"I'm sorry," Gabe says. "I'm just shocked to see Clarissa, that's all. Did you say you hired her Penny?"

"Umm... yes. Is that a problem?" Penny asks, her discomfort dragging on.

"Quite the opposite," Gabe says. He pulls out one of the spare chairs at the table and sits down. "Clarissa is originally from St. Augustine. She and I were best friends as children."

"Oh, small world," Penny says, her discomfort leaving her. She smiles at me. "You get extra points for not name dropping."

"Well in the interest of complete honesty I had no idea Gabe owned the bar," I say.

"What, even after seeing the name?" Gabe says before Penny can respond.

"Well, I did stop and think twice, and when I first came in, I half expected to see you behind the bar, but then I assumed Penny was the owner," I admit.

"So, you did remember?" Gabe says.

He looks at me and his gaze is intense and once more, I find myself looking back at him, unable to look away. I can feel my cheeks flushing pink as I nod.

"Of course, I remember," I say, surprised at how husky my voice sounds all of a sudden.

"That's good, because I remember everything," Gabe says. He smiles but I feel a shiver go through me as his eyes bore into mine. "Every dream we shared, and every promise."

"I do too," I say, my voice barely above a whisper.

4

GABE

I couldn't believe it when I saw Clarissa sitting in my bar with Penny. I had to blink several times before I allowed myself to believe it was really her. I should have believed it sooner because Clarissa had barely changed since she was a teenager. But it wasn't really the fact that she looked different or the same that had me not believing it was her at first glance. After so long of not seeing her, I barely dared to hope she had come back to St. Augustine.

She still has fair colored skin with a few more freckles, jet black hair and warm hazel eyes. Her hair has gone from hanging to her waist to being cut in a blunt bob with fashionable bangs. But I still couldn't mistake her, even with her change of hair style. I don't think you ever forget the girl who was your first love, and Clarissa was definitely mine, even if I never did get the courage to tell her so before her family moved away.

I've been sitting and chatting with Clarissa and Penny for about ten minutes now and it still feels surreal that Clarissa is here. As we chat, it gives me the strangest feeling. It feels like I have so much to catch up on with Clarissa, but at the same time, it feels almost like we've never been apart. I already feel so comfortable with her again, just like I always did.

I'd love for us to become as close again as we were then. Actually, I'd like us to become even closer than that. I let her get away one time and I don't plan on doing it again. But I'm getting ahead of myself. I don't know yet why Clarissa chose to come back home, and I don't know if she's married or has children or anything. I bet she is married though. I mean look at her. How could a woman so gorgeous not be taken?

As we've chatted, I've struggled to keep my eyes off Clarissa, and despite everything, she seems to be having the same trouble because our eyes keep meeting. It's probably just the novelty of seeing me after all these years for her, but I would love to let myself think it's something more.

"What brings you back to St. Augustine then Clarissa?" Penny asks when there is a slight lull in the conversation.

I had almost forgotten Penny was there as Clarissa and I talked. I would normally be annoyed at her for interrupting what I felt was a special moment for us but this time, I'm pleased because it's a question I've been dying to ask her but have avoided because I was worried it would have seemed too intrusive coming from me.

"Oh, the usual," Clarissa says. "My boyfriend cheated on me, broke my heart, and I decided to start over."

She says it with a casual shrug. She even gives a little laugh, but I can see the pain behind the laughter. It's something only someone who knows her well would see and while I'm not pleased that she's in pain – it's quite the opposite in fact - I'm pleased that I can still read her so easily. I have to admit I'm also glad she's single, although I'm angry at the bastard who hurt her. Angry and confused. Why would anyone have a woman as amazing as Clarissa is and throw it all away?

Penny is offering Clarissa her sympathy and an 'all men are bastards' type of line. I let it go on for a moment and then I decide enough is enough. I'm hardly going to throw myself at Clarissa, but I want her to remember that not all men are bastards. Namely, I'm not one. Or at least I hope I'm not one. I would never cheat on Clarissa that much is for sure.

"See there I was thinking you'd come back to town for the wedding," I say with a smile.

"What wedding?" Penny asks.

Clarissa snorts out a laugh and I know then that she remembers too. Mentioning it was a risk – if she had forgotten about it, I would have looked pretty pathetic but because we both remember it, that somehow makes it ok.

"Oh my God, you mean our wedding, don't you?" Clarissa says, still laughing.

Penny looks at her in open mouthed astonishment and her expression sets me off laughing too. Penny looks from Clarissa to me and then back to Clarissa again, seemingly unable to process what the hell she's just heard.

"We had one of those if we're not married by the time we're thirty, we'll marry each other pacts," I explain. "And I'm thirty now and Clarissa is a couple of months behind me."

Telling Penny about our pact brings it right back to the front of my mind and I find myself reliving the moment we decided to do it. We had been sitting in the bandstand in the park we always used to hang out in, keeping out of the rain. It had been mid-August and we were both dressed accordingly, the rain taking us by surprise.

5

GABE

"I'd like to get married somewhere like this one day," Clarissa said. "Imagine it. Rows of seats on the grass there, flowers intertwined in them and then the natural flowers and trees all around. And me and my man are in here so if it rained it wouldn't ruin my dress."

"Just everyone else's outfits," I laughed.

Clarissa nodded and laughed too.

"Yeah. It's my special day, not theirs," she replied.

I wanted to tell her it would be our special day, not just hers, because I should be the one she was marrying. I had loved the girl for as long as I could remember, and I couldn't imagine ever not being with her. The trouble was, I was well and truly in the friend zone. There was no way Clarissa felt the same way about me as I did about her. I knew that deep down, and yet, sometimes there were moments when I wondered. Moments when I caught her looking at me, or moments like now where the atmosphere between us seems to tingle. In those moments, I could let myself forget that she was like a million times out of my league. Or at least I could let myself think that maybe for a second, she had forgotten.

"It's probably not going to happen anyway, is it?" Clarissa said.

"Why not?" I asked.

"Well, what's the chances of me finding my 'Mr. Right' here in St. Augustine?" she said. Ouch. That one hurt me badly. "And I can't see someone who isn't from here agreeing to come here to get married."

"Right," I said, grinning at Clarissa. "Here's a proposition for you. How about this? You either get to marry the right man or you at least get to get married in your dream location."

"I don't get it," Clarissa said. "What do you mean?"

I smiled at her and got down on one knee and took one of her hands in mine.

"Clarissa Lydia Blayde. If we're not married by the time we're both thirty, will you marry me?" I asked.

Clarissa giggled and nodded her head and I stood back up and smiled at her. Her hand was still in mine, and I wondered for a second if I should risk kissing her. I didn't dare to do it though. It would ruin our friendship if she took offense to it. I would just have to play the really long game and hope Clarissa was still single when she was thirty. I didn't think for a second that would happen, but it was a nice dream to hold on to.

"It's good to have a backup isn't it," Clarissa said. I nodded, but her words hurt and judging by the way she frowned, I figured she'd seen the look on my face before I covered it with a smile. "Come on Gabe, as if it's even going to be a thing. You'll easily be married by the time you're thirty."

I wasn't sure how to feel about that statement. Did it

mean that Clarissa had only agreed to the deal because she was confident that she would never have to go through with it? Did it mean she thought I was marriage material? Was it both?

"RIGHT," Penny says, pulling my attention back to the here and now. "I'm going to get back to work. I'm afraid if I sit here any longer, you're going to try to rope me in as your wedding planner or something."

"Oh no, you're safe. We don't need a wedding planner. It's all planned. Fourteen-year-old me knew exactly what I wanted," Clarissa says.

She's laughing as she says it, but she's blushing slightly too, like she's embarrassed that she remembers so many of the details. She has nothing to be embarrassed about. I remember it all too; the white and dark purple color scheme she'd picked, the food trucks so we didn't have to have a fancy meal as she put it, the open-air disco after the actual wedding and then our honeymoon in Hawaii.

Penny stands up as our laughter fades away.

"I hope I get an invite to this wedding if neither of you find someone else in the next couple of months," she says.

"You'll be top of my list," I say.

"Oh no," Clarissa says, shaking her head. "She is literally the only person I know in town these days. She's my maid of honor."

"I like purple so why not," Penny laughs. "See you tomorrow, Clarissa."

She goes off back behind the bar and I smile at Clarissa.

"Can I get you a drink?" I ask.

"Yeah," she says. "I'll have my usual please."

I start to laugh, and Clarissa frowns her question at me.

"The last time I got you a drink, your usual was bubble gum flavored soda. I think you need to be a bit more specific," I laugh.

"Oh," Clarissa says, also laughing now that she understands the joke. "I'll have a pink gin and lemonade please."

I go to the bar and get her drink and I grab a bottle of beer for me. I go back to the table, hand Clarissa her drink and sit back down with mine. We clink our drinks together and take a drink. I nod to her glass.

"It's good to see your tastes have matured," I laugh.

Clarissa swats my arm playfully and laughs.

"What can I say? It tastes good," she says.

"I'm just joking," I say. "I like that you don't give a shit what anyone thinks, you just do your thing. I'm pleased that hasn't changed."

"It's funny," Clarissa says. "You think you've changed so much and then you come back to your hometown, and you realize you haven't changed at all."

"You say that like it's a bad thing," I point out.

"Well, isn't it?" Clarissa asks.

"I don't think so," I say, shaking my head. "Not when there was nothing wrong with you to begin with."

Clarissa smiles at me and I feel my heart flutter in my chest.

"You always were a sweetheart," she says.

"And I haven't changed and that's not a bad thing, right?" I say with a laugh.

She laughs too and then she shakes her head and turns serious for a moment.

"No. It's not a bad thing at all," she replies.

We go quiet for a moment, and I'm pleased that it's not an uncomfortable quiet that falls over us. It's the comfortable quiet of friends who can be in each other's company without being self-conscious. I'm glad we haven't lost that. Clarissa breaks the silence when she puts her hand over her mouth and yawns loudly.

"Am I boring you?" I tease her.

"Yeah," she says, nodding her head. "Totally."

She flashes me a grin that becomes a laugh and I laugh with her.

"Of course, you're not boring me," she says. "I'm just tired. I've had a long day sorting my apartment out and what not. I really should be making tracks and having an early night I think."

"I should probably get going myself," I say. That's not true. I have nowhere else to be but I'm not quite ready to let Clarissa go again right now if I have a choice in the matter. "I can drop you off at home. Or did you drive here?"

Clarissa shakes her head, and I don't know if that means no she doesn't want a ride or no she didn't drive here.

"I walked," she says. "But it's ok, I can walk back, it's not that far."

Oh, so she meant no to both then. I didn't even consider that as an option.

"I know you can walk back, but that doesn't mean you have to or that you should," I say. "Honestly I really don't mind."

"Ok, thank you," Clarissa replies with a wide smile.

She finishes the last of her drink and I do the same. She stands up and whisks my empty bottle and her glass up.

"I have to make a good impression right," she laughs, and she takes our empties back to the bar where I watch her exchange a few words with Penny.

I wave at Penny as Clarissa comes back towards me. She grins and waves back and as I gesture for Clarissa to lead the way out, I catch the raised eyebrow Penny is giving me. Nothing gets past Penny – she will have felt the chemistry in the air between Clarissa and me, I'm sure of it - and I know that I'm in for a lot of questions when I see her next.

We leave the bar, stepping out into the street, and I lead Clarissa towards my car. I unlock it and we both get in. I resist the urge to hold the door open for her. It feels too cheesy, especially when we're not even on a date or anything. If I was giving Penny a ride home, it wouldn't even occur to me to hold the door open for her and that's how I have to think of this. Clarissa and I are just friends, even if I want it to be more, and I still do. I want it to be more so bad.

"Where to?" I ask as I start the engine.

"Pipkin House please," she replies. "Over on Ninth Street?"

"Shut up," I say, unable to believe that this is just a coincidence. Penny must have told her to say that to freak me out or something. "Where really?"

"I really live there," she says. Her face falls slightly and she groans. "Oh God what's wrong with it?"

"Nothing," I say, shaking my head in shock. "I just can't believe that out of everywhere you moved into Pipkin House. I live there too."

Clarissa turns slightly to look at me, her mouth open in shock.

"No way," she says.

"Yes way," I laugh. "Number forty-seven."

"I'm number thirty-six. You must be on top of me," she says. Oh God, I wish I was on top of her. She's blushing again and I bite my lip, so I don't laugh when she corrects herself. "Your apartment must be on the floor above me I mean."

"Yeah," I say. The atmosphere in the car is so charged

after Clarissa's choice of words that I know I have to say something to bring us onto safer ground or I'm going to end up blurting out something I'll regret. "It's a nice place, quiet, you know. The people are friendly enough, but everyone mostly keeps to themselves."

"Thanks for the head's up," Clarissa says, smiling at me. "I know now to come to you if I need to borrow a cup of sugar or anything."

"Deal. You can have all the sugar you want," I say.

So much for me taking the sexual tension down a notch. We both know exactly what I meant by that, and Clarissa isn't screaming or trying to bolt out of the car so there's that. Still though, I do need to tone it down a bit. As much as I want her, I don't want to push her into something she's not ready for and I definitely don't want to be her rebound guy. I want to be sure she's well over this ex of hers before anything can happen between us.

I almost laugh out loud at that. Who am I kidding? Clarissa is being polite, that's all. The sexual tension is only in my head because I want it to be there.

6

CLARISSA

As I walk to work, I'm struck once more with the coincidences that have happened since I came back here yesterday. I mean talk about a small world. I managed to get a job in my old best friend's bar and then find out I live in the same building on the floor below him. I mean seriously what are the chances of that happening?

It's a good thing though. Having just moved back to town after almost fifteen years, I hardly have a bunch of friends lining up to spend time with me. I need all the friends I can get right now. I think I'll get along with Penny, but she'll be my manager and maybe that will make it weird socializing with her. Hopefully Rebecca, who I'm going to be working with tonight, will be someone I can be friends with.

Even if she is, it's still nice to have Gabe in my life again. He was my best friend for so long and I have to say our friendship is probably the most real friendship I've ever had, and I am so happy that we might be able to rekindle it.

I can't help but wonder what would have happened in my life if my parents hadn't decided to move to Europe when I was fifteen. Would Gabe and I be together now like an old married couple? Maybe we would be. I know he was into me when we were teens but back then I didn't feel anything more than friendship for him. But looking at him now, he definitely got hot somewhere along the line and when that happened, would I have started to like him back? Maybe I would have started to like him, and he would have given up on me by then. I could hardly blame him if he had.

Maybe we would have given it a go and maybe we'd have gotten our happily ever after. Or maybe we would have found that we weren't compatible and split up. To be honest, I think the latter option is the most likely. How many people seriously spend their lives with the person they start dating as a kid? It would be different if we were to start dating now, I think, because we're older and wiser and I'd like to think that we know each other well enough that if there was a problem we'd talk about it rather than let it fester away.

Anyway, I can't let myself think about that. It's lovely to have Gabe back in my life, but we can't be more than just friends. I can't trust any man, not even Gabe, at the minute, not after what Michael did to me. And I don't want to be in a relationship where I'm always second guessing everything. Especially not with Gabe. It would kill him to think that after everything, after knowing him for pretty much my whole life, I didn't trust him.

I reach the bar and quickly run my fingers through my hair, making sure it's in some sort of order. I pull the door open and step inside. A quick look around confirms that the bar is pretty quiet, but I think it'll pick up later on. I spot Penny grabbing some empty glasses from one of the tables. She sees me and smiles and nods towards the bar. We both head over there.

Penny spends the next half an hour or so sorting out my

paperwork and showing me how the cash register works, how the glass washing machine works, and where everything is. It's a simple enough set up – no taps, just bottles for the beers, standard spirits, that kind of thing. The cash register is easy enough to work and Penny reassures me that I won't be expected to settle up at the end of the night just yet.

She explains that she'll be working upstairs where there's a couple of private meeting rooms and I will be down here on the bar with Rebecca. I've served my first few customers, and everything is going well when the door opens, and a blonde woman walks in. Her hair hangs loose, the bouncy curls framing her face. She has pale green eyes that stand out even from this distance. She's tall and slim and my first thought upon seeing her is that she looks like a Hollywood actress. I can't put my finger on which one, but I don't suppose it matters. They have a type and she's the type.

"Here's Rebecca now," Penny says, nodding towards the glamorous blonde.

It is all I can do to keep from gasping to discover she works here. She comes over to the bar. She opens the counter and comes through, ducking through the door and out into the back. She returns a moment later minus her coat and purse.

"Rebecca, this is Clarissa. Clarissa, this is Rebecca," Penny says.

"Hi. Nice to meet you," I say with a smile.

"Likewise," Rebecca says.

She smiles too but it doesn't meet her eyes. I tell myself I'm being paranoid, but something tells me Rebecca has already taken a dislike to me. Well, isn't that just great. So much for her maybe being someone I could be friends with.

"Ok ladies, I have to go and get set up upstairs," Penny says. "Clarissa, if you need anything, just ask Rebecca, ok?"

"Ok," I agree.

Penny goes off and leaves Rebecca and me alone behind the bar.

"So," Rebecca says. I swear she's looking me up and down as she speaks but again, I try to tell myself not to be paranoid. "You're the wonderful Clarissa."

Ok so I'm not being paranoid. There's definitely something going on with me that Rebecca doesn't like.

"Huh?" I grunt, genuinely confused as to why she's taking this attitude with me.

"Gabe's old best friend? The one who can do no wrong?" Rebecca says.

Oh, so that's what this is about. She thinks I'm going to get special treatment because Gabe and I are friends.

"Yes, Gabe and I go back a long way. As for me being able to do no wrong, I very much doubt that's the case," I say. "Isn't Penny the manager? I'm sure she'll be quite happy to pull me if I fuck up."

"Yeah, to some extent, but even as the manager she's not going to want to piss off the owner's pet employee, is she?" Rebecca says with a fake innocence.

7

CLARISSA

I can feel my temper rising but I refuse to let her get under my skin.

Instead, I try to imagine how I would feel if I was in her position. In all honesty, I would probably think a similar thing to what she's thinking, but I wouldn't be threatened by it the way she seems to be, because I would be doing my job and not having to worry about being in trouble.

Is Rebecca so bad at her job that she fears it will become more apparent now that I'm here? Does she think I'm going to run to Gabe with information about her if she messes up? I decide to try and reassure her rather than letting myself get drawn into an argument with her. Maybe I can still salvage this and be friends with her. Maybe one day we will laugh at this moment together. I doubt it but who knows.

"Well as long as we just get on with our jobs and do what we're meant to be doing it won't be an issue will it," I say as calmly as I can.

Rebecca shrugs carelessly, but she doesn't argue the point. Fortunately, before either of us can say anything else, a customer comes up to the bar and I move to serve him cutting off the conversation.

When I've finished serving the customer, Rebecca has wandered off to the other side of the bar presumably to collect the empty glasses, although it looks to me more like she's just taking the chance to chat to the regulars. I don't mind. It's not like it's busy and I'm here to work. I'm not about to start making waves for anyone. Maybe this is Rebecca testing me to see if I will go running to Gabe and tell him about her taking advantage of me being here. Or maybe this is her way of training a new member of staff – disappear and see if they sink or swim. Hopefully I will swim.

Over the next hour or so, the bar gets gradually busier with both Rebecca and me serving customers at the bar and carrying out table service orders. Everything is going well but I can still feel that I'm getting the cold shoulder from Rebecca.

I've just served a customer with one of the rarer rums the bar carries and I'm trying to find it on the cash register, but I can't see it. I know I'm going to have to ask Rebecca where it is, as much as I don't want her to think I need her help.

"Rebecca?" I ask. She grunts rather than answering me in a civil manner but she turns her head in my direction and so I ignore her rudeness and just ask my question. "Where will I find the Santiago de Cuba Twelve?"

"Oh, it got missed off the rums when the cash register was being programmed," Rebecca says.

I wait for her to elaborate but it seems that's all she's going to say on the matter. I resist the urge to roll my eyes.

"Ok, so where did it end up instead?" I ask.

"Oh, I'm sure you can figure it out," Rebecca replies with a dismissive wave of her hand.

This time, I have to resist the urge to snap at her as well as wanting to roll my eyes. I try my best to keep my temper but when I speak, I'm sure she can hear the bitten back anger in my voice.

"I'm sure I can too but there's a customer waiting to pay, and I would rather him not have to wait ten minutes while I play 'hunt the rum' on seventeen different screens," I say.

Rebecca has turned away from me and she's standing chopping up a lime. I know she's heard me but she's going to pretend that she hasn't and I'm not going to give her the satisfaction of begging for her help. I start flicking through the screens when the customer speaks up.

"Jeez Rebecca what's up with you?" he says. He doesn't wait for an answer before he speaks to me instead. "It's on the miscellaneous screen, new girl."

I don't know if that's true or not, but it can't hurt to look there and when I do, I see it straight away. I don't press it. Instead, I turn around and smile at the customer.

"Thank you. This one is on me," I say.

"Oh, there's no need for that now," he says. "I'm a regular and I know where to find my own drink, that's all. I don't know what her problem is."

He nods towards Rebecca as he says it and I shrug and smile at him.

"I guess it's hazing the new girl time," I say, not about to tell him what I really think – that she's an insecure little bitch. "But seriously, the drink is on me sir."

"Thank you," he says, returning my smile and holding his glass up to me.

He leaves the bar and I duck through to the back and into the break room so I can grab the cost of the drink from my purse. I come back through to the bar and find Gabe standing talking to Rebecca. I feel my heart flutter when I see him, and I can't help but notice the tingling in my stomach even as I tell myself to ignore it.

"How are you finding everything Clarissa?" Gabe says as I ring the rum into the cash register and pay for it and put my change in my pocket.

"It's all good," I smile. "Nothing I can't handle."

I make a point of wording it this way, so Rebecca knows I'm not fazed by her silly games. Gabe nods towards the cash register where the receipt for the rum prints out.

"Are you sure? It's not looking good if it's got you hitting the hard stuff," he laughs.

I laugh too and shake my head.

"It's not for me. I gave a customer a drink on the house," I explain. Rebecca is glaring at me – I can feel her eyes boring into the side of my face - but I choose not to look at her. I could drop her right in the shit here, but I decide to be the bigger person. Maybe she'll cut me some slack when she sees I'm not going to be reporting everything back to Gabe. "It never hurts to get a regular or two on my side, right?"

"Right," Gabe agrees. "Well keep up the good work ladies."

He leaves the bar and I notice Rebecca watching him leave. Her eyes never leave him and that's when I know. She doesn't hate me because she thinks I'm going to run to Gabe about her or because she thinks I got the job unfairly. She hates me because she's jealous. She's into Gabe and she somehow thinks I'm going to stop her from being with him.

I want to tell her I've sworn off men for the foreseeable future. I also want to shake her and say look at yourself, you are smoking hot, I'm not a threat to you. I won't though. Not when she's been so hostile towards me. If she had been nicer, I might have reassured her, but she doesn't deserve my reassurance.

As Gabe reaches his group of friends, he turns back to look at the bar but it's not Rebecca he's looking at, it's me. I feel my cheeks flushing as tingles go through my body. I smile slightly and look down, feeling exposed by the intensity of our eye contact. I look back up and Gabe is still looking at me, his gaze even more intense. I feel the tingles flood through my body again.

8

CLARISSA

"Hey new girl," a voice says from the other side of the bar. I force myself to look away from Gabe and focus on the customer with a smile. "Rumor has it that you're giving away free drinks."

"Oh, the rumors are greatly exaggerated," I laugh.

"Not to worry. Pretty girl like you, we should be the ones buying you drinks," he says. "I'm Geoff by the way."

"Hi Geoff, I'm Clarissa," I say.

"Clarissa," he repeats and then he spends a moment seemingly considering my name. "I like it. It suits you."

"Thanks," I say. "So, what can I get you?"

"Are you on the menu?" Geoff asks with a grin I'm sure he thinks is sexy but is actually a little bit creepy.

I keep my tone light when I reply to him, but I'm aware that he's gone a step too far and I don't want to harmlessly flirt with him and give him the wrong idea.

"Nope," I say. "Just the usual drinks."

"Oh, I know why," Geoff says. "The drinks are all cold, and you are hot."

I flash him a quick smile because I'm not sure what else

to do or say that wouldn't be seen as rude. He smiles back and asks for a vodka and soda which I quickly make him. I put it on the bar in front of him and he hands me a ten-dollar bill.

"Keep the change," he says.

"Thanks," I say, forcing myself to smile at him.

"Hey Clarissa," Geoff says as I put his change in my tip jar. "Does that get me your cell phone number?"

"I don't think so," I say, trying to laugh off his request.

He laughs too and I think he might be joking but then he shows me he isn't.

"Oh, expensive girl huh? Next time I'd best pay with a twenty-dollar bill," he says.

He winks at me and saunters away from the bar. I shake my head slightly and then I look up and find Gabe looking from me to Geoff. His face is full of thunder, and I feel another tingle go through my body. Is he jealous? It sure looks that way, but I tell myself I'm being silly and get back to work.

By about ten thirty, the bar has a good atmosphere, but the crowd is starting to dwindle down and we find a bit of a lull at the bar. I busy myself with filling up the bottle fridges and Rebecca starts cleaning down the drip trays on the bar.

"Did you and Gabe used to date?" Rebecca asks me out of nowhere.

"No," I reply. "It was never like that with us. We were best friends."

"But you wanted to date him, right?" Rebecca says.

I shake my head.

"No. Like I said it wasn't like that. Did you want to date your best friend growing up?" I ask.

"Well, no, but my best friend was a girl," Rebecca replies.

"So?" I shrug.

"Ok, point taken," Rebecca says. "I just wanted to be sure because I don't want to step on anyone's toes. You know because there's this chemistry between Gabe and me."

"Right. Well, you've got nothing to worry about there," I tell her.

I'm not sure where this chemistry is that she thinks they have but whatever. She obviously likes Gabe and if it makes her feel better to think he likes her too then who is she hurting?

I happen to glance up at that moment and I instantly catch Gabe's eye where he's watching me again. Again, I feel my skin tingling under his gaze and I feel my pussy throb with want. I have to stop feeling this way every time he looks at me. I need a friend so badly right now, not a boyfriend or a fuck buddy.

"Yeah. It looks like it," Rebecca snaps icily before she flounces off to collect some glasses.

I guess she caught the look that happened between Gabe and me. It's funny how she seems to think that it's only me that's into him and not the other way around. I mean he has to be staring at me for me to look up and catch his eye. It's not like I'm instigating it either. I sigh. I guess I just have to accept that Rebecca and I are not going to be friends. I can live with that. Who needs a friend that is so much hotter than you anyway I think with a smile to myself.

I finish putting fresh bottles into the fridge, stopping occasionally to serve a customer. I smile at Penny as she appears beside me.

"How has tonight gone then?" she asks me.

"Good," I reply. "I've definitely got a feel for things and none of the customers complained. Or at least not to my face."

We both laugh and Penny confirms that no one has complained to her either.

"Did you find everything ok?" she asks me, and I nod. "Good. I don't want to overwhelm you by showing you the settling up procedure or how to secure the place. It's almost time for last call, you can go now. We're all covered for tomorrow, so how about we see you Sunday evening? Seven o'clock again?"

"That's great, see you then," I reply, surprised that I'm not being asked to work tomorrow with it being Saturday but I guess Penny will already have the main night covered.

I head out to the break room to collect my things and as I do I debate calling a cab, but I decide against it. I'll walk home. It's barely a five-minute walk and it's not like St. Augustine is a dangerous place to walk around. I come back to the bar area and duck through the hatch.

"See you Sunday Rebecca," I say, trying to make the effort with her even though I can't help but feel that I'm the newbie here so it should be her trying to make the effort.

She grunts in response. I suppose it's better than her outright ignoring me. I wave to Gabe who is once more looking in my direction. He raises his hand, returning my wave, and I head outside. The contrast between the heat of the bar and the cool of the night hits me and despite it being rather mild really, I pull my jacket tighter around me and cross my arms over my front.

I duck into the alley beside the bar. I'm about a quarter of the way in when I become aware of footsteps behind me. They are getting closer, and I can hear someone breathing too. The hairs on the back of my neck stand up. Am I being followed? I start to move a bit quicker, telling myself not to panic, just to keep moving.

"Clarissa. Wait up," a voice calls from behind me.

I don't recognize the voice, but it must be someone who knows me for them to know my name. I feel much better to think that whoever was following me was only doing so to catch up with me. I slow down and glance over my shoulder to see Geoff hurrying towards me.

"You slipped out without saying goodbye," he says as he catches up with me. I open my mouth to apologize although I don't really think I'm expected to go around the bar and say goodbye to all the customers before I leave work. The apology dries up in my throat when Geoff goes on. "And you still didn't give me your cell phone number either. Don't think I'm going to just let you run off into the night without me having it."

I give an awkward laugh and I start walking a bit faster. We are about halfway through the alley now and once we are clear of it; I only have two or three blocks to go and I'm home.

"Hey, slow down," Geoff says, his voice slightly slurred from the alcohol he has been drinking.

I don't slow down, hoping maybe Geoff will take the hint and stop pushing for something I'm clearly not comfortable giving him. Instead, he grabs my arm and drags me back towards him a bit. I try to pull my arm free of him, but he has a good grip on me.

"What are you doing? Get off me," I say.

"Don't be so uptight," he replies, still holding my arm. "You were going too fast that's all."

"Ok, I'll slow down," I say.

He still doesn't release my arm and I try once more to pull it away.

"Stop it you fucking tease," Geoff says. "What, you think you can flirt all over me and then just walk away when you're done? I don't fucking think so lady."

With that, he wrenches my arm backwards so hard I think my shoulder is going to pop out of its socket. He slams me against the wall and presses his body against mine. He grabs my wrists and pulls both of my arms above my head. He grips both of my wrists in one large hand. I take a deep breath and yell.

"He-," I shout

It's as far as I get. The "lp" is stifled by one of Geoff's sweaty palms being slapped across my mouth. He leans in closer to me and hisses into my ear.

"Shut the fuck up," he says. He goes from threatening to playful and back again in the blink of an eye, but where I was afraid of him when he was threatening me, the playful thing is actually worse. It makes me feel nauseous and it makes me realize he isn't going to stop because he has somehow convinced himself that I want him like he wants me. The constant shift of attitude also throws me off balance and I don't know what to say to get through to him. "You know you want this. You don't have to play hard to get with me."

He bucks his hips and I feel his hard cock pressing against my ass through his jeans. Fear takes over me as he releases my wrists and starts trying to push my dress up. I try my best to push him away now that my hands are free, but he is stronger than me and I can't budge him. He moves his hand to his own crotch, and I hear his zipper open. Hot tears spring from my eyes and run down my face.

I try to scratch at his face, and he grabs my wrists again pushing me harder against the wall so that I can barely move. I don't even move the half inch or so I can move because every little movement makes me feel his cock again. He thrusts, his cock banging off my ass cheek. I whimper and he does it again, seemingly driven on by my fear. He presses one of his hands over my mouth again before I can even gather enough wits to call out.

"Put your palms flat on the wall," he says close to my ear.

I shake my head. I am not going to make this easy for him. He seems to sense that, and he goes back from playful to threatening once more.

"Put your fucking palms flat on the wall or I will make you do it," he says.

Still, I resist him and then he wraps his hand up in my hair and drags my head backwards. I know what he's going to do. He's going to slam my face against the wall. I quickly lift my hands to the wall and push my palms against it.

"See. That wasn't so hard was it," he says. "Now don't move them or you know what you'll get."

I hear the rustling of denim as he pulls at his fly once more and I close my eyes, silent tears cascading down my face once more as I anticipate what he is about to do to me.

9

GABE

I 've found it so hard to keep my eyes off Clarissa tonight. I'm fascinated by her. The way she moves, so graceful and sure of herself, the way she smiles and laughs, the way she pushes her hair back off her face, I want to see it all. Just watching her turns me on like I never would have believed and every now and again, I'm rewarded by her smile or by her catching my eye and holding my gaze for a second or two longer than what I would think of as normal. Whenever that happens, I allow myself to think that maybe, just maybe, something could happen between us.

I wanted nothing more than to go over to her and kiss her. I kept imagining what she would taste like, what she would feel like in my arms. I had more than once imagined myself ripping her dress off and lifting her onto the bar and making love to her. I wanted to do just that so badly but of course I restrained myself.

I had been ready to start throwing my regulars out in the street when I saw several of them flirting with Clarissa over the course of the night and I had to remind myself that it meant nothing. Clarissa was a beautiful woman – people were going to notice that, and they were going to try their luck with her, but to her, they were just customers. She smiled and played along but any good bartender will do that. I knew as well as she did that it meant nothing. It still sent a jolt of pain through me every time I saw it though.

She's gone off somewhere now and I find that I can concentrate on the conversation my friends are having a little bit easier now that I haven't got Clarissa distracting me.

"Oh, you want to talk to us now do you?" Matt laughs and the group laughs with him. It's not unkind laughter but I have no idea what he's talking about, and I frown which makes Matt laugh even more. He goes on when he's finally stopped laughing. "Good god man you don't even know you're doing it do you?"

"Doing what?" I ask.

"Watching that new bartender. I can't decide whether you like her or whether you think she's about to rob the cash register," Matt laughs.

"It's complicated," I sigh. "Do you guys remember me telling you about my best friend, the one I was head over heels in love with?"

"Holy shit, that's Clarissa?" Ben says, his jaw dropping.

"Yup," I reply. "And believe it or not, she's even hotter than she used to be."

"So, get in there and ask her out," Matt says. Ben and the others are nodding along with him. "You're not kids anymore. She might feel the same way."

I shake my head.

"She's just got out of a relationship where her ex cheated on her. If I'm going to be with her, I want to be with her because she wants me for the long haul. I don't want to be her rebound guy," I say.

"I don't know if that's such a bad thing," Ben says with a

grin. "The rebound guy gets all of that hot, angry at the world sex."

"That's not what I want. I want hot, let's spend forever together sex," I say.

"Well, if you've waited for what, almost fifteen years? I'm sure you can wait until she's done the rebound thing and is ready to settle down again," Matt says.

I nod, but the thought of Clarissa with someone else makes me feel sick, so I don't dwell on it for too long. Matt nudges me and nods towards the bar. I glance over and Clarissa is exiting the bar with her jacket and her purse. She sees me looking over and waves. I return her wave and then I force myself to look away from her. I don't want her thinking I'm some weirdo who watches her every move. I mean I am that weirdo I just don't want Clarissa to realize that.

The conversation moves on to Matt's thirtieth birthday party which we are having in the bar tomorrow night. Everything is already sorted and arranged, and I'm looking forward to the night. I already was, but now I'm even more so because it looks like Clarissa is going to be behind the bar.

I suddenly remember that Clarissa hasn't got a car unless she went and bought one today which I highly doubt. I know obviously that our apartment building is only a five-minute walk away from the bar, but I still don't like the idea of her walking home alone at this time of the night.

"I'm going to call it a night," I say to the others.

This announcement is met with laughter and a few whooping sounds.

"Why's that? Just because your eye candy has gone?" Ben teases me.

I laugh along with them. If I try to deny it, I know it will only make it worse. I say my goodbyes and hurry out of the bar. I start towards the parking lot to get my car, planning on driving until I spot Clarissa and then picking her up. I'm almost at the parking lot when I realize she won't be walking down the main street and then around the long way. She'll have cut down the alley beside the bar and then she'll walk down through the park, so I turn and head down the alley.

As I turn and head the other way, I'm jogging lightly, confident I can catch up with Clarissa if I hurry up a bit. The alley is dark compared to the front street which is well lit, and I'm conscious of not wanting to turn an ankle or end up falling into a pile of garbage so I slow down slightly until my eyes adjust to the darkness. Once they do I start jogging again.

Up ahead, I can see what looks like the outline of two people. At first, it looks like they're getting a little bit carried away with each other and I'm feeling a bit uncomfortable at the thought of passing them, like I'm a dirty old man watching them getting it on or something. As I get closer though, I realize that my first assessment was wrong.

There are two figures, a man and a woman, but there is nothing about this that suggests the woman is wanting the man on her. He has her pressed up against the wall, her hands pressed onto it and her body bent at the waist. I think it was this position that made me at first assume the woman was wanting this. But now I see that the man has one of his hands over her mouth as his other hand tugs at his fly. And I see a sparkle of light through the otherwise darkness that surrounds the woman's face which I assume must be tears that are dripping from the woman's eyes.

I stop jogging and start sprinting. I can't just stand by and watch this happen. I don't even consider the fact that the man could be armed or that I could be running into danger. I'm angry in an abstract sort of way. Like what right does this man have to do this to someone? As I get even closer, my abstract anger becomes an intense and personal anger that drives me faster. The woman is no stranger. It's Clarissa. My Clarissa. And this creep has his filthy, unwanted fucking hands on her.

"Get the fuck off her," I shout.

The man looks up and I feel my jaw drop in surprise. This is no opportunistic stranger. This is a regular – Geoff I believe he is called - from my bar who has followed her out here.

I reach the pair of them and swing my fist hard. It connects with Geoff's jaw and his head flies to the side. I feel a stinging pain in my knuckles where my fist connected with bone.

"What the fuck man?" Geoff shouts, his hand going to his face and resting there where I hit him. "She wanted this as much as I did."

One glance at Clarissa's tear-stained face tells me that's not the case and I swing for Geoff again. I catch him in the nose this time and he stumbles backwards several feet. He loses his footing and falls to the ground, his now flaccid penis like a small white worm against the dark color of his jeans.

"Don't even think about coming back to The Black Swan," I say. "You are barred for life."

Geoff doesn't reply as he tries to zip himself back up. I hold my hand out to Clarissa who takes it quickly and I walk her past Geoff, making sure that my body remains between the two of them so there is no chance of him reaching out and grabbing her, not that I really think he would dare try that again.

10

CLARISSA

I don't stop walking until we're out of the other side of the alley into the well-lit streets again and then I stop and hold her out at arms' length. She doesn't look like she's been hit or anything but she's still crying softly and that alone breaks my heart.

"Are you ok?" I ask, then I shake my head. "No. Stupid question. Of course, you're not ok. I mean did he hurt you? Do you need to go to the hospital or anything?"

She shakes her head.

"I... he grabbed my wrists. They're a bit sore but I don't need to go to the hospital or anything. I was just so scared. I really think if you hadn't come along when you did, he would have... he wasn't going to stop," she says, fresh tears spilling down her cheeks.

I swallow hard, trying to swallow down my anger at the bastard who did this to her. I pull her into my arms and hold her tightly. She instantly wraps her arms around me, and she rests her head on my chest. I can't help but notice the strawberry scent of her hair. I can't help but love the feeling

of her warm little body against mine. In any other circumstances, I would definitely be debating kissing her, but I'm
not a complete bastard. I don't want to save her from one
asshole for me to become another one. I just hold her until
she pulls back and looks up at me.

"Thank you," she says.

"Of course," I shrug.

We start walking again and Clarissa slips her arm
through mine. I love the feeling of her hand on my arm. She
sends goosebumps rushing over my skin from where she
touches it and it's becoming harder not to kiss her. I
continue to stop myself though.

We reach our apartment building. I unlock the door and
hold it open for her. She goes inside and ignores the
elevator and goes to the stairs. I shrug and climb up the
stairs with her. We reach the third floor and Clarissa smiles
at me.

"I guess this is goodbye then," she says. "Thank you
again."

"Oh no, no way," I say. She frowns and I smile. "I am a
proper gentleman. When I escort a lady home, I must escort
her right to her front door."

I pull open the door that leads away from the staircase
and into the hallway. Clarissa giggles but she doesn't object
as she ducks through the door, and I follow her. We reach
her front door, and she looks down at her purse, presumably looking for her keys. It's then that she gasps.

"Oh Gabe," she says. She reaches down and takes my
hand in both of hers, lifting it up between us. "You're
bleeding."

"Oh, it's nothing," I say, shrugging off her concern
despite the fact that my hand is stinging quite a bit.

"It's not nothing at all," Clarissa says. "Come on in and I'll clean it up for you."

"Honestly, that won't be necessary," I insist, although the thought of going into her apartment with her makes my pulse speed up.

"Nope," Clarissa says with a smile. "I am a proper lady, and I will take care of any gentleman who gets injured whilst defending my honor."

"Ok, fine, you got me," I laugh, giving in gracefully.

Clarissa nods, pleased with herself. She goes back to rooting through her purse and finds her keys. She unlocks the front door and nods towards another door.

"Go on in and make yourself comfortable," she says. "I'll go grab some stuff to treat your hand. Do you want a drink?"

"Sure, if you are," I reply.

She goes off and I go through the door she indicated and step into her living room. I take my coat off and hang it over the back of an armchair and I wander over to the mantel and take a look at some of Clarissa's ornaments and photographs. I pick up a photo frame and run my fingers over the glass on a picture of her and her mom standing side by side, smiling identical grins. I put it back down and move on, smiling when I see the next photograph.

The photograph is of a baby I don't recognize but what makes me smile is the silver dove on the frame. It's the frame I bought for Clarissa for her sixteenth birthday and ended up giving it to her as a going away present when her family moved to Europe. And after all these years, she still has it.

"You bought me that frame. Do you remember?" Clarissa says from behind me.

I hadn't even heard her come in. I turn to face her and nod and smile at her.

"I do," I say. "You got it early. It was meant to be for your birthday."

Clarissa is sitting on the couch now. She's putting down all the things she has brought in with her. A bottle of red wine and two glasses have been nestled underneath her arm. In one hand, a bowl of antiseptic. In the other hand, a bag of cotton balls and a tube of some sort of cream. She pats the cushion beside her.

"Come and sit down," she says.

I make my way over towards her as she opens the wine and pours two good size measures. She hands me one of the glasses and smiles at me.

"To friendships, new and old," she says.

I clink my glass against hers and we drink. She puts her drink down and starts fiddling with the bag of cotton balls. I put my drink down too when she finally gets the bag open and dips the first cotton ball into the antiseptic. I hold out my hand, palm down. Clarissa places one hand underneath it, her palm facing up. As she lightly presses her palm against mine, I hear her suck in a breath and I feel tingles pulsing up my arm.

The very air around us feels charged and I know if I kissed Clarissa now, she would kiss me back. But I also know I would forever wonder if she only kissed me back because she felt like she owed me something for helping her earlier. I don't want to be seen as some sort of opportunistic predator, so I resist the urge to kiss her once more. It's getting harder and harder to do though.

Clarissa has started to dab my knuckles with the wet cotton ball now and I grit my teeth against the pain.

"Sorry," she says.

"It's fine," I tell her.

She looks up at me and smiles and our eyes meet and

once more I feel the magic in the air. I clear my throat, unsure of what to say or do to diffuse the tension. Clarissa looks back down at my hand and I blurt out the first thing that comes into my head.

"Who is the baby?" I ask.

"What baby?" Clarissa says.

I nod towards the mantelpiece.

"The one in the photo," I say.

"Oh, that's Callum, my best friend from Italy's baby. He'll be about eight now," she says.

"He's cute," I say.

"I know," Clarissa agrees. "And he was always such a sweet baby, always smiling and laughing."

She seems to be finished cleaning my hand now and she dabs it dry with a clean cotton ball and then she spreads some of the cream on it. The cream stings a little bit, but I barely notice the sting with the feeling of her gentle fingertips rubbing my hand.

"All done," she says with a smile.

I don't want to move my hand away from hers, but at this point, it'll be weird if I don't and so reluctantly, I move my hand away. I look over my knuckles and smile up at her.

"That feels so much better, thank you," I say.

She smiles again and then she picks up her glass and leans back on the couch. I pick up my glass too, but I stay sitting forward although I turn slightly to the side so that I'm looking at Clarissa.

"Are you feeling better now?" I ask her.

I don't want her to dwell on what happened or keep reminding her about it, but I also don't want to go up to my own apartment and then find out she was scared or upset after I left her.

"Yes, I'm feeling much better now thanks," Clarissa says

with a smile. "I mean I know it could have been a lot worse, but you came along at the right moment and I'm not going to dwell on how bad it could have been. I guess I have to stop thinking that nothing bad can happen here. Maybe I'll get some pepper spray."

"Or let me know when you're leaving and I'll give you a ride home," I say.

"I can't ask you to do that every time I'm at work," Clarissa says.

"I know. But you're not asking. I'm offering," I say.

"That's just semantics," Clarissa laughs. She turns serious again. "But don't worry. I've learned my lesson. I'll be walking the long way around on the main street from now on."

I don't bother to argue the point with her. She isn't going to agree to using me like a cab service I know that. But now I know she'll be walking along the main street instead of cutting through the alley way, I know I can just hop in my car when I see her leave and pick her up like I planned on doing tonight.

I don't want to overstay my welcome here and I figure Clarissa might be tired after working tonight so I finish my drink and smile at her.

"Well, I best be getting off then. Thanks for the drink and the first aid," I say as I stand up.

Clarissa stands up too as I put my jacket on and then she walks me to the door.

"See you tomorrow night then yeah," I say as I step out into the hallway.

Clarissa shakes her head.

"No. Penny said there's a party, but everything is covered tomorrow. I'm back on Sunday night," she tells me.

"It's Matt's party. My friend," I say. "Come to the party with me."

I blurt out the invite before I can talk myself out of it. I want her to come with me but if I had time to think about asking her, I would have thought it over completely and made it into an 'is this a date or not' scenario and then I would've been nervous and weird.

"Oh no don't be silly. I don't want to intrude," Clarissa says.

Despite her words, I know she wants to come. I know her. If she didn't want to come, she would have just said no, not the part about intruding.

"How will you be intruding?" I ask. "It's my bar, remember?"

"I know but turning up at a party I'm not invited to. Isn't that kind of intrusive?" she says.

"No. You can be my plus one," I tell her. "You'd be doing me a favor in a way. All my friends will have their wives and girlfriends with them and for once, I won't be the odd one out."

That's not strictly true. Most of my friends will be bringing a date, that much is true. The part about me worrying about being the odd one out is a lie. I really don't care. In fact, I have kind of given up on finding a long-term relationship with someone because everyone I even consider dating, I measure against Clarissa, and none of them could even match up to the imagined version in my head. There's no chance of any of them matching up to the real version now.

"Well, ok then, but only if you're sure," she says.

"I'm sure," I say. I smile but I hope I manage to keep it to a normal smile. In truth, I want to smile so wide my face hurts. I want to do a little dance and jump into the air. "I'll stop by for you around eight?"

"Eight is great. See you then Gabe. And thanks again for tonight," Clarissa says.

I give her a half wave that I could kick myself for because even as I do it I know it's lame and then she closes the door and I punch the air and walk off the happiest I've been in years.

11

CLARISSA

I pull my blue dress down slightly as my doorbell rings. I grab my purse and head for the door, telling myself that I'm feeling butterflies in my tummy because I'm excited to be going to a party, not because I'm excited at the thought of seeing Gabe again.

I open the front door and there he is. He's wearing dark blue jeans and a cream-colored t-shirt. His cologne moves towards me, a faint but enchanting scent that makes me think of the outdoors somehow. I breathe it in, breathe him in. I look at his face and see him looking me up and down.

"Wow," he breathes. "You look stunning."

He smiles at me then and I can see the tiny lines around his eyes, his glasses making them a little bit more pronounced. Laugh lines. Smile lines. And now he's smiling because of me.

"You scrub up well yourself," I say.

I step out into the hallway and close and lock my front door. I drop the key into my purse. Gabe holds his arm out to me, and I link my hand around his elbow.

"Car or walk?" Gabe asks me as we reach the ground floor of the building.

"Car if you don't mind," I say. I nod down to my feet, my black strappy shoes with the high, spiky silver heel. "I don't mind walking home because I'll have had a drink and I'll take my shoes off, but I can't do that on the way there."

Gabe laughs and leads me out of the back door of the building into the parking area. We get into his car, and he drives us to the bar.

"Who's this Matt then?" I ask. I've been curious about him since I agreed to go to the party. "I would have thought I'd know him if he's from here and he's our age, but I can't think of a single Matt I remember from school or anything."

"Matt didn't grow up here," Gabe says. "He moved in with his girlfriend here. You'll know her. Savannah Mitchell."

"Oh Sav. Wow I haven't thought about her in years," I say. "How is she?"

"Good," Gabe says. "She's seven months pregnant with her second child."

I smile to myself. Sav always wanted a big family. It's good to know she's making a start on it.

We reach the bar and Gabe parks, and we get out of the car. He offers me his arm again and I take it and we walk around to the entrance. We walk in still arm in arm. The first thing I notice is the daggers Rebecca is throwing at me with her eyes. The second thing I notice is a mixed group of people all elbowing and nudging each other, nodding and smiling in our direction.

"What's going on?" I ask Gabe when it becomes obvious to me that they're talking about us.

He looks a bit embarrassed as he turns to me and explains.

"When we were kids, I had a bit of a crush on you. You know that right?" he says.

"I kind of suspected," I admit.

"Right. Well, I've made the mistake over the years of telling the guys about you. And now you're back and I think they have bets on how long it will take before I ask you out," he finishes.

I have to bite my tongue to stop me from blurting out the question I want to ask him – when is he going to ask me out? – I don't want that. I've sworn off men. Instead, I just roll my eyes and laugh.

"And they say women are bad for gossiping," I say. "Come on, let's go get some drinks and then we'll go and face the music."

Gabe nods and we go to the bar. He orders a Jack Gabes and Coke for himself and a pink gin and lemonade for me. I smile to myself, secretly pleased that he remembered my drink order. Once we have our drinks, he leads me over to the group.

"Hi everyone, this is Clarissa," he says.

A man wearing a large badge with the number thirty emblazoned on it steps towards me and takes hold of my shoulders. He air-kisses my cheeks and I laugh and play along.

"So, you're Clarissa then huh?" he says.

"And I'm guessing you're Matt?" I reply. "Happy birthday."

"Thanks," Matt says.

Another man steps forward. He looks me up and down and then smiles at me.

"Pleased to meet you, Clarissa. I've heard *a lot* about you," he says.

He puts the emphasis on a lot and the group laughs. I smile sweetly and then give as good as I got.

"I'm sorry, I didn't catch your name," I say sweetly.

"Ben," the man says.

"Ben. Ok. Then I'm afraid I'm a little bit on the back foot here because you know lots about me, but Gabe hasn't mentioned you at all, so I know nothing about you," I say.

This gets an "ooh" and a laugh from the group. Even Ben laughs. He slaps Gabe on the shoulder.

"She's a keeper man," he says. "She's as good at keeping me in my place as my own girl." He nods at a pretty, dark haired girl who rolls her eyes but smiles at his words. "Clarissa, this is Kelly."

Kelly and I exchange hellos and I'm introduced to a few more people. At some point Sav comes back from the bathroom and she and I spend some time catching up. We move to one of the bigger tables and all squeeze around it. I find myself between Gabe and Sav which is good. Sav and I chat and chat, and I start to feel like I've never been away from St. Augustine.

As another glass of pink gin and lemonade appears in front of me, I realize that this must be my fourth or fifth drink and I haven't been to the bar once. Oh God does this mean Gabe will think this is a date? Will he think I just let other people pay my way for me? Neither of them are great prospects. I turn to Gabe.

"I'm so sorry," I say. "I was just caught up in the conversation. Let me get the next few rounds, ok?"

Gabe laughs and I frown.

"I'm serious," I say.

"I know you are," he replies. "But it's an open bar Clarissa."

"Ohhh," I say and then I laugh. "Well in that case you can remain on bar duty if you want to."

I'm surprised and a little bit sad to learn that Gabe knew all along this wasn't a date. I'm also annoyed at myself for feeling this way. I should have just felt relief.

"Oh my God," Sav shouts suddenly, grabbing my arm and pulling me to my feet. "I love this song. We have to dance."

I allow myself to be pulled up from the seat and over to a clear area and Sav and I start dancing. I put my arms up, my hips swaying to the music. Kelly, and two of the other girls, Maria and Shauna, join us and when the song finishes and the next one starts, none of us make any move to sit down.

"So, are you and Gabe like together now?" Maria says into my ear, shouting slightly to be heard over the music.

We're still dancing as we talk, and I shake my head in answer to her question.

"But it's only a matter of time though, right?" she says.

"I'm not really looking to get into anything," I say. "I've sworn off men. My last boyfriend cheated on me and I don't want to risk getting hurt again."

"Yeah, but I'm willing to bet your last boyfriend hadn't been in love with you for like fifteen years before he did that," she said.

"Gabe isn't in love with me," I say. "He had a bit of a childhood crush on me all of those years ago but that's it."

"Yeah right," Maria laughs. She studies me for a moment and stops laughing. "Wow you're serious, aren't you? You really don't see it."

"That's because there's nothing there to see," I say.

"God girl you couldn't be any further from the truth if you were in Alaska. Just watch him. You'll soon see it for yourself. He can hardly take his eyes off you," she says.

I shake my head, but I can't help but think that she's kind of right. Not about Gabe being in love with me – of course he isn't – but about how he keeps looking at me. He was doing it yesterday when I was working, and I know he's doing it now. And I'm not ashamed to admit that I might be swaying my hips a little bit more provocatively than I usually do when I can feel his eyes on me.

I can't feel his gaze at the moment, and I casually look around. Since we got up to dance, more people have followed our lead and the bar is jumping. I can't see our table through the moving bodies.

"Oh, trouble incoming," Sav says, nodding back in the direction of our table.

She moves to the side and the rest of us follow her and I see we now have a clear path of vision to our table. And Rebecca is making her way towards it.

"Ugh she's so desperate," Sav says. "The way she's all over Gabe all the time. It's cringe worthy. Honestly Clarissa, I kind of want you two to get together just so I don't have to watch her pitiful attempts at getting him to notice her."

"Watch, she's going in for a quiet word. But then what?" Shauna giggles.

I feel a strange sense of dread in the pit of my stomach as Rebecca leans down and speaks into Gabe's ear. I hate to say I recognize the feeling as jealousy, but I do. I don't know why I'm jealous. It's not like Gabe is my boyfriend. It's not even like I want him to be my boyfriend.

Rebecca straightens back up. She laughs and flicks her hair, the perfect curls bouncing around her face. Gabe smiles at her, a strained smile that looks like he's just trying to be polite. Rebecca puts a hand on his shoulder and then she starts to squat down. I realize what she's doing at the same time as Kelly blurts it out.

12

CLARISSA

"She's going to sit on his lap," she says.

She was definitely trying to do just that, but Gabe manages to slide out from beneath her just in the nick of time and she ends up just sitting in the chair he has vacated. I can't help but laugh along with the other girls. Gabe says something to her and then moves away from the table. With the show over, we go back to dancing.

I feel a hand on my hip as I move and I'm just about to slap it away, the memory of being touched by a stranger last night still fresh in my mind, when Gabe's voice whispers into my ear and I relax.

"May I have this dance?" he says.

"You're such a nerd," I say laughing and turning to him.

"But that's a yes though, right?" he says.

"Yes, it's a yes," I smile, and we start to dance together.

Gabe takes my hand and twirls me around. He pulls me against him and then I twirl away. We spin and shimmy and giggle and I'm having the best time. I don't even let it bother me when I make accidental eye contact with Rebecca, and she glares at me like she wants to throttle me here and now.

After a few songs, Gabe whispers in my ear that he's going to the bar. I tell him I'm going to the lady's room, and I'll see him back at the table. I tell the girls the same thing and I make my way across the crowded, makeshift dance floor and to the bathroom. I go in and go into a stall. I've just sat down when the girl in the next cubicle taps lightly on the wall and then speaks to me.

"Hi. Sorry to bother you. You don't have a spare tampon, do you?" she says.

"Umm I might, let me check," I say. I root through my purse until I find one. It's a bit bashed but it must be an emergency for the girl to ask so I shrug my shoulders and lean down to hold it underneath the stall wall. "Sorry it's a bit bashed. I only use this purse when I go out, so it's been laying around in there for a while."

"Oh, don't worry, thank you so much. You're a literal life saver," she says.

I finish my business and as I'm pulling my dress down, I realize it's not just this purse I haven't used in a while. It's tampons in general. I try to think of the last time I had a period, and I can't at first. I'm still thinking as I flush the toilet and leave the stall and make my way to the sinks to wash my hands.

It comes to me that it was definitely more than three weeks ago. My cycle is usually pretty regular so that must mean I've missed a period. I'm not overly surprised to be honest. The stress of what Michael did to me and then the stress of moving and everything. These things take their toll. I tell myself I'll do a pregnancy test in the morning just to rule it out, but I'm not worried.

I dry my hands and then look into the mirror above the sink. I apply a bit of lip gloss, and I'm putting it back away in my purse when I see movement behind me in the mirror.

Rebecca comes into the bathroom. I force myself to smile at her when our eyes meet in the glass.

"Hi Rebecca," I say.

"Hi Rebecca," she repeats in a squeaky voice.

I'm shocked. I know she doesn't like me, but I didn't expect her to be so blatantly rude.

"What the fuck," I snap. "What's wrong with you?"

"Oh, come on now, don't play 'little Miss Innocent with me'," she says, looking me up and down. "Do you think I didn't see you with those girls laughing at me?"

I feel myself blush. She's right. I shouldn't have been laughing at her. I'm not the sort of person who wants to make anyone feel bad about themselves and Gabe's rejection of her must have stung enough without her seeing us all laughing at her too.

"I'm sorry," I say, meaning it. "That was pretty nasty of me."

Rebecca shrugs her shoulders.

"Whatever. I'm over it," she says. She doesn't sound over it but I decide that's not a helpful thing to say and so I don't say anything. Rebecca heads towards the stalls but before she goes into one, she turns back to me. "Those girls are bitches. You might think they are your friends, but trust me, they're laughing at you behind your back as well."

I don't really know what to say to that, but Rebecca goes into the stall without waiting for an answer. I'm not sure if that was her attempt at an olive branch, a warning for me not to get too close to these women because they're so cliquey, or whether it's just her last-ditch attempt to make me feel crappy because I made her feel crappy earlier on.

I leave the bathroom and I soon forget about Rebecca altogether when Gabe spots me and beckons me to him. I feel myself smile as I realize what song is playing – "Fallin" by Alicia Keyes. It was the song I told Gabe I wanted as our wedding song back when we made our pact. I remember it so well because Gabe told me it wasn't a wedding song because she kept falling in and out of love and in a wedding song, the couple should surely stay in love, and I told him I didn't care, it was a beautiful song, and it was what I wanted.

I make my way over to Gabe and he pulls me into his arms, and we sway to the music.

"You remember," I say.

"I remember," he confirms. "But it's still the worst wedding song choice in the world."

We both laugh and I shake my head.

"Nope. I'm not having that," I say. "It's a lovely song and it's more accurate. Like it doesn't try to make marriage easy. There will be ups and downs. Alicia knows the crack."

Gabe laughs again and I raise an eyebrow and try to stay serious, but I can't do it and I end up laughing too. As I stop laughing, I shake my head slightly and a strand of my hair sticks to my lip gloss. Before I can reach up and remove it, Gabe's hand is there. He moves the hair and then he caresses my cheek, and we look at each other, our eyes meeting.

I search Gabe's eyes and I can see the truth of a potential relationship with him, but I still don't know if I'm ready to let anyone in and I don't want to start something only to realize I wasn't ready and lose Gabe from my life altogether. Even as this all goes through my mind, I can feel myself leaning in to meet Gabe as he leans into me. Our lips are less than an inch from touching when I hear giggles and hands pull me away from Gabe.

"Sorry Gabe, this is a girl's anthem and we're stealing Clarissa away," Sav laughs.

It's only then that I realize that Beyonce is now singing

"All the Single Ladies". I hadn't even noticed that the song had changed. I hadn't noticed anything except how good it had felt to be wrapped up in Gabe's arms. I'm disappointed to be pulled away from him, but I allow it to happen all the same, and the rest of the night goes by in a blur of drinking and dancing and laughter. I spend most of it alternating between wanting Gabe to kiss me and reminding myself that I've sworn off men for a long time.

I sit on the closed lid of the toilet. The time is passing by so slowly as it always seems to do when I have to wait for something. This time, I'm waiting for my pregnancy test to be ready to show me the results. I feel as though I should be nervous, but truthfully, I'm not. I mean seriously, what are the chances of me being pregnant?

I've worked it out and the only time I've had sex since my last period was that time Michael came over and I embarrassingly threw myself at him. Surely, I can't be that unlucky that I could get pregnant off that one time. I think it's much more likely that I've skipped a period because of all the stress in my life.

I make a promise to myself to make an appointment with a doctor when I get a chance and talk to them about the possibility of taking something to make me feel a bit less stressed if things don't improve. I also vow to help myself a bit by eating better, exercising more and getting plenty of sleep. That should all help me to feel better and get my cycle regular again.

I check my watch again. Twenty more seconds to go. I sit and watch the second-hand creep around in its slow, teasing circle until it's time and as I reach for the stick on the side of the sink, for the first time, a flutter of nerves does hit me. What will I do if I'm pregnant?

"Oh, get a grip, you're not bloody pregnant," I say out loud and I smile to myself, my uncertainty over.

I reach out and pick up the stick and I feel my stomach clench with nausea as I see the results: pregnant.

13

GABE

I can hardly keep the smile off my face thinking about last night at the party. Clarissa and I danced, and we chatted, and we laughed and several times we almost kissed. I genuinely believe that if we hadn't been interrupted by Savannah and the others, we definitely would have kissed that last time.

If I had kissed Clarissa when I had walked her back to her door, I'm confident she would have kissed me back. She might even have invited me into her apartment and let me make love to her. I resisted the urge though because by then, she was more than just a little bit tipsy, and I didn't want to take advantage of her. If anything ever does happen between us, I would hate to think that Clarissa woke up the next day and regretted it.

When I left her last night, I asked her if she would be ok, and she reassured me that she would be. Or at least she would be as ok as she could be with a hangover from hell. She confessed that her method for getting over it was to drink lots of coffee until around four and then eat greasy fast food. I hope she meant it because I'm going to look really stupid when I knock on her door with burgers and fries if she didn't mean it.

I knock on her front door before I can change my mind. I wait for her to answer. It's taking a while and I'm about to give up when she finally answers. I open my mouth to ask her how she's doing but the words dry up in my throat when I see that she has been crying, and recently judging by the wet skin beneath her eyes. There's obviously something very wrong here and it's something much worse than a hangover.

"Clarissa? What is it? What's happened?" I ask.

"I..." she starts but then her voice breaks and she just shakes her head as fresh tears fall.

I step forward and embrace her, holding her as her body shakes with sobs. I rub my hand up and down her back and make soothing noises. Her sobs start to trail off into hiccups until finally, she does a big sniffle and then she steps back out of my arms and wipes at her face.

"I'm sorry," she says.

"Don't be," I reply. "What happened?"

"Come in," she says, stepping away from the door. "I'm sorry I should have said that sooner."

I step inside and close the door behind me and then I follow her through to the living room where we sit side by side on the couch. We sit the same way we did after I walked her home from work on Friday but this time, it's very different. It's obvious she's still upset, and I want to help her, to make everything better, but I don't know how to because I still don't actually know what's wrong.

"Is that McDonald's I smell?" Clarissa says after a moment of silence.

I nod and hand one of my bags of food to her. She peers inside and moans in appreciation. She rips the bag and puts it on the coffee table in front of her. She unwraps her burger and takes a bite and then she eats a fry. I start to eat my own meal too. We are about halfway through the meal when Clarissa smiles at me. It's a strange smile because while her lips look happy, I can still see the pain in her eyes.

"So, I guess I owe you an explanation about the state I was in when I opened the door," she says.

"You don't owe me anything Clarissa. If you don't want to tell me something, you don't have to, but I would like to help you in any way I can if you do want to tell me what's happened," I tell her.

She looks down into her lap and gives a bitter sounding little laugh.

"I don't think you can help me with this one unless of course you have a time machine," she says.

"Not right now but I'm working on it," I say.

She looks up and smiles and I can see the little sparkle in her eyes trying to make a comeback. I'm glad that I can still make her smile, even when she's clearly upset.

"I'm pregnant," Clarissa says.

I have to admit I was not expecting that at all. Does she think the baby is mine? Is that why she was so hesitant to tell me? I know I'm being ridiculous. We've never slept together, and Clarissa obviously knows this, but it's just the strange direction my mind went in for a second.

"I... wow," I say after a moment. "My usual response to that would be congratulations but I don't think that's right here."

"It's not," Clarissa says. "God, Gabe, what am I going to do? The last thing I want right now is a baby. I don't have enough money to even support a baby. I have barely settled in here and I don't have the spare room for a nursery or any of the million and one other things a baby needs. But I can't get rid of it. I just... I can't. I don't think it's right for me to abort my child because it's inconvenient for me to have it now."

"What about the father?" I ask. "Will he be around to help you?"

"I think it's fair to say the chances of that are pretty slim considering I'm not going to tell him about it," Clarissa says. I raise an eyebrow and she sighs. "Don't get all judgy on me. The baby is Michael's. My cheating ex. I don't want him in my life and I'm not going to give him the chance to abandon my baby or hurt him or her like he hurt me."

"I wasn't being judgy I swear," I say. "I was just surprised when you said you wouldn't be telling him that's all. Not because I think he has any right to know or any rights to the baby at all, just because well, wouldn't he have to contribute to the baby financially?"

"He would, but I would rather end up homeless and starving than take a penny from that bastard," Clarissa says.

She says it with such conviction I know that she means it. But there are still options for her to consider.

"What about adoption? Would you consider that?" I ask.

"I don't know," Clarissa says. "I mean in theory, yes, it's the perfect solution. But you hear all these stories don't you, of kids stuck in the system and I don't want that for my child. And then there's the time when they find out they are adopted, and they have all of these abandonment issues. It feels like the same as an abortion really – like it's a cop out that makes things easier for me whether it's the right thing to do for the baby or not."

"That doesn't sound like an I don't know Clarissa. That sounds like you've made your mind up to keep the baby," I say.

"I suppose I have," she says. "And we'll be ok. Once I calm down a bit and get used to the idea, I can start making real plans. I'll have to take on another job alongside the bar of course. Maybe two. Then I might be able to afford a two-bedroom apartment at least."

I picture Clarissa working herself to the bone, exhausted and sick of her life, working three jobs just to be able to afford to feed and clothe her baby and then getting caught up in that trap of having to work more hours to pay for childcare and then needing more childcare because she's working more hours, and I know that I can't sit back and see that happen to her. I know she doesn't want me romantically and I have long ago made my peace with that, but it doesn't stop me from loving her. And when you love someone, you help them where you can.

I take a deep breath and Clarissa looks at me strangely.

"What's wrong?" she says. "You look all nervous all of a sudden. Don't worry I'm not planning on leaving the bar and leaving you in the lurch."

God if only that was my biggest fear. I laugh and shake my head.

"It's not that," I say. "It's... well... I think I might be able to help you."

"Oh, I know you're going to help me," Clarissa says with a smile. "Uncle Gabe is going to be Babysitter-In-Chief."

I laugh and Clarissa joins me, but her laughter doesn't have the usual musical twang to it.

"Actually, I was thinking of something a bit more permanent. Like being a dad rather than an uncle or a babysitter," I say.

"I don't understand," Clarissa says with a frown.

"Marry me," I say. Clarissa's jaw drops so far I can almost picture it bouncing off the ground and I let her shock work to my advantage because she is too shocked to say no yet, so I hurry on before she can outright reject the idea. "It makes perfect sense. You're my best friend; we get on so well and I know I will love your baby like it's my own. I can give you security. I promise I will take care of you and your baby."

"But... what's in that for you?" she asks.

Oh, seeing you every day. The hope that one day, you'll see me as more than just your best friend. That's what I think, but it's not what I say.

"Why does there have to be something in it for me? I told you I would help you if I could and I can," I say.

"It's too much Gabe. I can't ask you to give up your entire life to help me. What about when you want to find a wife that isn't just in name? What about when you want to have kiddies of your own?" Clarissa says.

"I hardly call living with you giving up my life. You're not that bad," I say, trying to lighten the mood a bit.

Clarissa laughs but then she's serious again.

"But the rest of it. What happens when you regret this moment?" she says.

"I won't regret it," I say. "Look Clarissa, I know myself and I know this will make me happy. And I hope it will make you happy in the sense that you will be safe and cared for. I'll be honest. I've given up on the whole meeting the right girl and having babies thing. At least this way I'm no longer the weirdo single guy and I won't have people constantly bugging me about when I'm going to settle down. You'd almost be doing me a favor."

"I don't think I'd go that far," Clarissa laughs.

"Well how about this – it would be mutually beneficial to the both of us," I say.

14

GABE

We fall quiet and go back to eating but I can see that Clarissa is thinking about what I've said. Since I've explained it in more detail, she still hasn't out right said no yet. I feel like she wants to say yes but she's afraid that she is asking too much of me. I wish I could tell her I love her to the moon and back and nothing would ever be too much. But I don't want to scare her off and I certainly don't want her to feel like she owes me some sort of relationship because I'm helping her out.

I know if I can just find the right thing to say, I can get her to agree to this. I know it's unconventional but when we made our pact all those years ago, I meant it. I wanted to marry Clarissa one day and I still do. And as for the baby? Well, whatever happens I can love the baby too. It's half Clarissa and that's enough for me to know it will be an awesome kid.

I finally fall into a thought that I think might help her to make her decision. This thought, I'm more than happy to vocalize.

"I should make you aware this is a one-time offer," I say.

"It's like one of those blue light sales. Once it's gone, it's gone."

"So, you're telling me I have a limited time to make a decision this big about my future?" Clarissa says.

From anyone else, that would sound like a bad thing, a complaint. But I know Clarissa and I can see her lips wanting to curl up in a smile and her stopping them so that she can be all pretend serious.

"Yes. That's what I'm telling you. You have thirty seconds to make up your mind," I say.

"Thirty seconds? Really," Clarissa laughs.

"Ding ding. Time's ticking away," I joke. "Just twenty-six seconds left. Oh, would you look at that. Twenty-five seconds left."

She laughs and nudges me with her elbow.

"Seriously Clarissa, think about it if you need to, but promise me that you will think about it as a serious option," I say.

"Do you really mean it?" Clarissa asks.

I look straight into her eyes and nod. She seems to see the truth in my eyes because she doesn't push the point.

"There would have to be some ground rules," she says.

"Like?" I prompt her.

"We would have to have separate bedrooms," she says.

"Obviously," I reply, although I'd love to share a bed with her. "I have a three-bedroom apartment so that won't be a problem. A room each and a nursery."

"No cheating," she says. "No, that's not right. I guess it wouldn't technically be cheating if our marriage isn't real. But no seeing other people. I know it's a big ask but I don't want to be seen to be one of those dumb ass wives who is being cheated on and doesn't notice. I've been there once, and I won't go there again."

"Done," I tell her.

"You're that sure?" she says.

"I'm that sure," I reply. "I totally get what you're saying, and it works both ways. I don't want to look like a fool either so no men for you."

"Agreed," Clarissa says.

Score. Maybe she'll never really fall for me but at least I won't have to watch her with someone else. I know that even thinking such a thing makes me a selfish bastard, but I can't help how I feel.

"Anything else?" I ask.

"There is one more thing. And it's the biggest thing and I need you to promise me you will do it no matter what ok?" she says.

"I promise," I tell her.

"I haven't told you what it is yet," she points out. I shrug and laugh, and she nudges me with her elbow again. "Be serious for a moment. I need to know that if at any point the arrangement starts to bother you, or if you start to resent me, or anything like that, the second you don't want to do this anymore I need to know, ok? I won't be mad. I'll just be grateful for what you've done for me - for us – up until that point."

"I promise," I say again.

She looks into my eyes again, and once again, I feel like she's searching for my truth. Once again, she seems to find it because she smiles and I see her visibly relax, the tension leaving her shoulders and letting them sag down a little bit.

"Ok. Ask me again," she says.

I smile at her and get down on one knee in front of her. She laughs but she doesn't insist I stop so I go on.

"Clarissa Lydia Blayde, you are my best friend and I love

you to the moon and back. Will you do me the honor of becoming my wife of convenience?" I ask.

She laughs again but I'm sure I see tears forming in the corners of her eyes before she blinks them away.

"I will," she says.

15

CLARISSA

I swallow hard as the nerves suddenly start to overtake me. I didn't expect to be nervous. It's not like this is a real wedding as such. It's just Gabe and me going through the motions and it's hardly a society wedding where there are tons of people. There are a handful of people, most of whom I don't even know.

We both decided against inviting our families because it would just be too hard to explain the situation to them and without that explanation, I know how they would react. I think both sets of parents always wanted Gabe and me to grow up and get together and they would think we'd finally done it if they came to the wedding. I mean we have finally done it but not in the way they would think.

I think the nerves are coming from the fact that I'm still not sure if this is a good idea or not. There's no middle ground with it. I know that much. It either works and it's the best plan ever or it fails and it's the worst plan ever. I'm just hoping for it to be the first one.

I never imagined myself marrying someone for anything but love and I'm sure Gabe would say the same about himself. It's not too late to call the whole thing off I suppose but even the idea of being a single mom terrifies me. I just can't do it on my own.

"Ready?" Penny says, smiling at me. "The car is here."

I nod and smile at Penny and Sav, both of whom agreed to be my bridesmaids at very short notice. They are wearing matching dark purple color dresses, their bouquets purple and white like my own. I wasn't going to get a wedding dress, I was just going to get a nice evening gown, but then I saw the one I'm wearing, and I just couldn't resist it. It's made from white satin, the bodice part more netty. It's tight fitting in the right way, accentuating my curves and skimming over my hips. I have to admit that I feel like a million dollars in it.

We get into the car and the car heads towards the park. It is literally a minute's drive. I insisted we could walk but Gabe wouldn't hear of it. He told me I was getting the wedding of my dreams and that didn't involve a twisted ankle. He was right about that much, and, in the end, I gave in gracefully.

The car drives into the park and follows the little road around until the area for the wedding comes into view. Gabe and Penny have taken care of everything, and I gasp when I see how beautiful they have made everything. All the chairs they've pilfered from who knows where – most likely the bar – have been covered in white fabric with purple bows on them. The ends seats have white and purple flowers intertwined together and the band stand is completely decked out in the same flowers.

The car gets as close as it can to the area, and we get out. Sav and Penny take a moment to sort out my veil and the back of my dress. As they do, I take a quick look over the guests. I spot Ben and Kelly, Shauna and Neil, Maria and her boyfriend whose name escapes me. I also spot Rebecca which surprises me but she's sitting with a group of people including Zac and Riley both of whom I've met this week who work in the bar. I get it. Gabe could hardly invite all the staff from the bar except her could he.

The girls have finished fussing with my dress and with a subtle nod from Penny, music begins to play. I look up at Gabe standing up in the bandstand with Matt, his best man, beside him, and the minister opposite them. I'm not one for religion for the most part, but I always talked about a minister when we talked about our wedding at thirty simply because back then I didn't realize you could get married without someone other than a minister outside of Las Vegas.

I can't keep the smile from my face when I recognize the song playing – it's "Fallin'" of course. Gabe hasn't let me down on one single detail, even down to him and Matt wearing ties that match the bridesmaid's dresses.

I feel a funny sort of rolling feeling in my stomach, like butterflies but a bit less fluttery. I don't have a word for the feeling except it feels like... no. I can't be falling in love with Gabe. Just because he has remembered all this stuff and literally planned the wedding of my dreams doesn't mean I'm going to fall in love with him. Just like the way he looks in his suit, so elegant and handsome doesn't mean a thing. He is hot though. Fuck me, is he hot.

Penny and Sav pick up the bottom of my dress at the back and I lift the front slightly as I climb the steps onto the bandstand. Gabe holds his hand out to me, and I take it and I feel that feeling again as my skin tingles against his, but again I tell myself that none of this means anything. None of it is even real. I'm just letting myself get caught up in the act. There's just something about a wedding that brings out the romantic side of me, especially so it seems, my own wedding.

"Ready?" the minister asks and Gabe and I both nod. He smiles and then he looks up and addresses the guests. "I would first of all like to take a moment to welcome you all to the wedding of Clarissa Lydia Blayde and Gabe James Kerrey." He pauses then looks down at his bible on the lectern in front of him. He reads then looks back up and recites it to the guests. "Love is patient. Love is kind. Love is not envious or boastful or arrogant or rude. It does not insist on its own way. It is not irritable or resentful. It does not rejoice in wrongdoing but rejoices in the truth. It bears all things, believes all things, hopes all things and endures all things. God is love and those who live in love live in God and God lives in them."

The minister carries on, reciting a prayer and talking a little bit more about God and love and I'm starting to feel like a fraud, but I remind myself that I do love Gabe. I really do. He's still my best friend. And surely God doesn't differentiate between types of love. Gabe must sense my turmoil because he squeezes my hand and when I look at him, he mouths 'are you ok?' at me. I nod and smile reassuringly at him, calmed by his touch. I push my doubts aside and tune back into the minister's words.

"Firstly, I must ask if anyone knows of any lawful reason why these two people cannot marry to declare it now," he says. He gives a dramatic pause and part of me is waiting for Rebecca to jump up and start singing that old song, 'It Should Have Been Me'. She doesn't of course and the minister goes on, his focus on Gabe and me now. "The vows you are about to take are to be made in the presence of God who is judge of all and knows all the secrets of our hearts.

Therefore, if either of you knows of a reason why you may not lawfully marry, you must declare it now."

I almost blurt it out then, just admit to the minister that it's all a sham, but I bite my tongue. He didn't ask for any moral revelations. He asked for lawful reasons why we can't marry each other and there are none of them. I think I just let the heavy shit about God knowing all my secrets get into my head for a second there. I'm glad I'm not into religion. I would be a nervous wreck all the time. It's so intense. The minister seems to have decided we've had long enough to confess anything we might know, and he goes on again.

"Gabe, will you take Clarissa to be your wife? Will you love her, comfort her, honor and protect her and forsaking all others, be faithful to her for as long as you both shall live?" he says.

"I do," Gabe replies and despite myself I feel a warmth spreading through me at his acceptance of me.

The minister repeats the same question to me and without hesitation I tell him that I do. And I will. That's all stuff a best friend does to some extent, and we've already discussed the forsaking of all others thing. He then repeats the questions a third time, this time asking the congregation if they will support us. They chorus back their "I will," and I know at least one of them is lying but in this present situation, who am I to judge?

The minister does another prayer and then he asks the congregation to sing a hymn. Considering how small the so-called congregation is, this is deeply embarrassing for all involved and I'm glad when the song comes to an out of tune end.

"And now for your vows. In the presence of God and your nearest and dearest you may face each other," he says.

Gabe and I turn until we are facing each other, and Gabe

takes one of my hands in each of his. He smiles at me, and I know somehow that we are doing the right thing. That whatever comes next, in this moment, we have made the right decision.

"Repeat after me," the minister says to me. "I, Clarissa, take you, Gabe, to be my lawfully wedded husband."

I repeat the line and we go through each of the vows line by line until both of us have sworn to the other to be there for each other in sickness and in health, for richer or for poorer, till death do us part and all that jazz.

"And now for the exchanging of the rings," the minister says. Matt and Sav both step forward, Matt handing a ring to Gabe and Sav handing a ring to me. "Let these rings be a symbol of unending love and faithfulness and a reminder of the vows that have been sworn on today."

The minister smiles and nods to Gabe. Gabe takes my left hand in his and smiles at me as he pushes the ring onto my finger.

"Clarissa, I give you this ring as a symbol of my love for you. Just like the ring never ends, nor does my love for you. All that I am, I give to you. All that I will ever be is yours for all eternity. I love you," he says.

Saying personal vows wasn't something we had agreed on and I feel myself choking up at his words. The fact that he has taken the time to say something personal, something from the heart, tells me that he doesn't regret this for one minute and that means more to me than I think he will ever know. I smile at him with teary eyes, my vision blurring slightly as I take his left hand in mine and push the ring onto his finger. I don't want to just do the standard vow now that he has made the effort and I smile at him, nervous again.

"Well, I don't have any fancy words planned," I start,

which gets a smattering of quiet laughter from the congregation and a smile from Gabe. "But I want you to know that the moment I gave you this ring, you became nothing less than my everything."

Gabe squeezes my hand again and the minister has to gently prize our hands apart so that he can carry on which gets another laugh from the congregation.

"In the presence of God and before this congregation, Gabe and Clarissa have given their consent and made their marriage vows to each other. They have declared their marriage by the joining of hands and by the giving and receiving of rings. I therefore declare them to be husband and wife," the minister says.

A cheer goes up from the little crowd and they applaud, and their warmth and applause make the crowd feel not so little anymore. The minister takes our right hands and puts them together and Gabe and I smile at each other as we cling to each other's fingers.

"Those whom God has joined together, let no one put asunder," the minister says. He drops our hands and takes a step back. "You may now kiss your bride."

This is a moment in the ceremony I've been looking forward to and dreading in equal measure. I've been looking forward to it because a few times now Gabe and I have come so close to kissing and there is always that tension around us, that chemistry. It'll be interesting to see what, if anything, I feel when I kiss him in a controlled way that won't be awkward or weird because it's just expected. I'm dreading it in case I don't feel anything, and he does. Or in case I feel the earth move and he doesn't.

Or in case it's just as awkward as all hell.

Then Gabe smiles as he moves in towards me and when our lips do touch, I'm no longer in my head. I'm very much in my body and I feel the sparks of electricity go shooting through me where Gabe's lips touch mine. Suddenly it doesn't feel like I'm kissing my best friend just because it's the right thing in this situation. It feels very much like a kiss being shared by two lovers.

My lips tingle and I can feel my clit pulsing, my pussy getting wet. My nipples are erect, and my face is flushed. I wrap my arms around Gabe, and he holds me tightly against him. I'm sure he must be able to feel the hardness of my nipples against his body. Our kiss deepens and I can feel myself falling into him.

A light coughing sound brings me back to the moment and I suddenly remember where I am and that we have a full-on audience. Gabe breaks away at the same moment as I do, and we look at each other and start to giggle.

"Erm. Yes. Right then," the minister says, obviously made a little bit uncomfortable by our kiss. "Let's go off and sign the license."

Gabe and I follow the minister and Matt and Penny, our witnesses, follow us. We all sign the license and it's only when that is done that I notice that while I've been distracted, a food truck has pulled up, a mobile bar has appeared beside it, and a disco has been set up.

"Is this ok?" Gabe asks as we stand at the top of the bandstand steps for a second.

"It's perfect," I tell him, and it is. It really is.

As we step down the steps and are received by our waiting guests, it strikes me that I'm not afraid anymore.

16

GABE

I smile at Clarissa, and she smiles back at me. I still can't believe that this gorgeous woman is now my wife. I was determined not to think of it that way because I know it's not a conventional marriage. Clarissa is my wife on paper, and I intend to support her, but I told myself that I could never let myself believe there was anything more to it than that. But then there was that kiss.

That kiss that was just – oh my God – it was everything. I felt my whole body come to life as Clarissa's lips touched mine and I felt sparks flying through my whole body. But it was more than just that though, more than just the physical side of it. For those brief few moments, I felt what it would be like to have Clarissa love me back and for those brief few moments, I allowed myself to think it was a possibility that one day she might love me like I love her.

Now all I can think about when I look at her is that kiss. I can't help but have my gaze linger on her lips and I can't help but remember how she felt in my arms, her breasts against my chest, the heat from her body encompassing me.

"Are you ok?" Clarissa asks me.

"Never better," I say with a smile. "Why do you ask?"

"I don't know. You keep smiling," she says.

"Right. A sure indicator that something is wrong," I reply with a laugh.

"You know what I mean," Clarissa says.

"I'm just happy at how the day went and I'm looking forward to our honeymoon," I tell her.

We talked about the idea of a honeymoon and while we both agreed it probably wasn't necessary, we also agreed that it would be nice to have a few days away somewhere. Clarissa doesn't know where we're going – I wanted to organize it all as a surprise for her. We're going to Hawaii where we'll be staying in a two bedroom suite in a five-star hotel complete with its own spa. She's going to love it.

"Me too," Clarissa says. "To both of them. I'm intrigued to know where we're going."

"You'll find out soon enough," I say. I glance at my watch to confirm the time. "We'll be getting picked up in half an hour or so."

"I still can't believe we actually did it, waited until we were both thirty and got married," Clarissa says.

"Is that you can't believe it in a good way I hope?" I ask.

"Yeah of course," Clarissa smiles. "You don't regret it do you?"

"Not even a little bit," I say. "I even organized the wedding to fall on your thirtieth birthday so there was no chance of you marrying someone else."

We both laugh at that and then Clarissa turns serious. She looks me in the eye, and I feel my cock tingle.

"There's no one else I would rather be married to than you," she says. "It all feels like it was meant to be, you know?

You came back into my life at a time when I needed you so badly even though I didn't know it at the time, and you stepped up for me."

"I'll always step up for you," I say, meaning it.

Any trace of laughter has left us. The atmosphere around us feels loaded once more. I can almost see the sparks of electricity shining blue and silver in the air. My breath catches in my throat as Clarissa moves closer to me on the couch and tilts her face up to mine. I don't need to be asked. I lean down to meet her, and our lips come together once more.

This time, there's no holding back. We kiss like we're starving, and the other person is food. We devour each other's mouths, our tongues colliding and wrapping around each other, our hands roaming over each other's bodies. I can feel my cock hardening as Clarissa runs her fingernails lightly down my back underneath my shirt.

I push one hand into her hair, pressing her lips more tightly against mine. She moans into my mouth and presses her body against mine. I run my other hand down her side and onto her hip and then I run it up and down her thigh. I want to move closer to her center, play with her clit and make her feel amazing, but I don't want to rush her into something she might not be ready for.

I needn't have worried. After a second or two of my running my hand over her thigh, she grabs my hand and pulls it up, pressing it against her mound. She lifts herself enough that I can pull her leggings and panties down. I get them to her knees, and she lowers herself again and I push my fingers between her lips.

She's warm and wet and slippery, everything I imagined she would be and more. I move my fingers through her slit until I reach her clit and then I begin to massage it, slowly and steadily at first. I take my cues from her, upping my pace as her breathing gets louder and more affected.

She shifts slightly so that her legs can open further giving me better access. I don't waste this gift, using the extra space to rub her in a figure eight shape. She starts to move her hips, upping the pace of my massaging of her and she grinds down on my hand, pressing herself tightly against me.

She moans into my mouth, and I keep moving my fingers as I kiss her. I move them faster and faster, and Clarissa pulls her mouth from mine and rests her head on my shoulder. I can feel her warm breath tickling my neck as she gasps and pants as I put her through her paces.

Her clit is practically pulsing beneath my fingers now and I know she's so close to coming. She takes in a long, staggered breath and then she holds it, tightening her grip on my body and pulling me closer to her. At the same time, she presses her thighs closed, pressing my fingers tightly against her.

I feel a rush of warm, wet liquid cascade from her as she makes a whimpering sound. Her lips clench around my hand and her back arches, lifting her head from my shoulder. I can see the tendons standing out on her neck and I can see the way her face is contorted with ecstasy. She sucks in a breath and whispers my name over and over again.

I feel my cock pulsing in time with her whispers and hearing my name in that low, husky voice of hers makes me want to come on the spot. I hold myself back though. I don't want this to end that way.

I feel the moment that Clarissa's orgasm ends. Her rigid body loosens and the grip of her lips on my fingers relaxes.

Her head flops back down onto my shoulder as she pants for air.

"Holy shit," she says after a minute.

She lifts her head up and kisses me again before I can respond to her declaration. She pushes her tongue into my mouth and makes an "mmm" sound like she is savoring the taste of me. She runs her hands over my body and the next thing I know, she's unbuttoning my jeans. Just as she is about to reach in and grab my cock, my cell phone buzzes loudly. I pull my mouth away from Clarissa's.

"Fuck," I say, not needing to look at the screen of the cell phone to know who is messaging me. "That's our ride."

"You're kidding me," Clarissa says, pulling back from me. I shake my head and she chuckles. "I guess I'll have to owe you one then."

She jumps up and pulls her panties and her leggings back up. I moan in frustration as I refasten the button on my jeans and stand up.

"I'll hold you to that," I say.

"You best make sure you do," she laughs as she flits towards the door.

Did she just let me know that this isn't the end of our physical relationship? I don't want to jump to conclusions or set myself up to disappointment, but I can't help but think that that's exactly what she meant.

I readjust my jeans, having trouble finding a comfortable spot for my cock. My jeans feel too tight around it wherever it sits, and I know I just have to accept that I'm going to be like this until it goes down.

I follow Clarissa into the hall and take her suitcase from her and then I pick mine up in my other hand.

"Can you lock the door?" I ask. "My keys are in my shirt pocket."

She gets the keys out and I feel her fingers brush my nipple. It springs to life beneath her fingers, and she giggles.

"Someone's happy to see me," she says.

I don't think I need to tell her at this point that my nipple isn't the only part of my body that's pleased to see her.

We get out of the apartment and Clarissa locks the door and pops my keys back in my pocket. We go down in the elevator this time. A woman is already in there and we all politely greet each other. I wish Clarissa and I were alone in here so I could steal a kiss from her.

We go down to the lobby and get out of the elevator. I put our cases into the trunk of the car and Clarissa gets into the cab. I get in a moment later.

"The airport please," I confirm with the driver.

"So, are you going to tell me where we're going yet?" Clarissa asks me.

"Ok," I say. "We're going to be staying in a suite at the Montage Kapalua Bay Hotel."

"I don't know where that is," Clarissa says.

"Oh, that's a shame then. You'll have to wait and see," I say with a laugh.

"Noooo," Clarissa says. "You can't get my hopes up to know like that and then just change your mind."

"Well, I can because I just did," I point out.

"That is so not fair," Clarissa says, still laughing. "Do I have to tickle it out of you?"

She goes for my ribs, and I duck away laughing. I hold my hands up in mock surrender.

"Ok. Ok. You win," I laugh. "It's in Hawaii."

Clarissa's jaw drops.

"Seriously?" she says.

I nod and she squeals in excitement and throws her arms around me and for that reaction, the hotel was worth every dollar, even if it did take a fair chunk of my savings to pay for it.

17

CLARISSA

"Thank you," I say, smiling at Gabe as he turns his head towards me and opens his eyes.

"What for?" he asks.

"Everything. All of this," I say, gesturing around us with my hand.

"You deserve it," he says with a shrug and closes his eyes again.

I lay back on my own sun lounger and close my eyes too. I still can't really believe we're here. The hotel is absolutely stunning, the sun is shining, and this place is everything I could want from a honeymoon.

We walked down to the beach this morning and spent a couple of hours sunbathing and swimming in the sea. After that, we wandered around a few shops and then we stopped for lunch in a lovely little terraced café. After lunch we went on a lovely long walk and then we came back to the hotel for an hour or two around the pool and then we had dinner. After dinner, we came back up to our suite and came out onto the balcony to lay on the loungers there and soak up the last few rays of sun.

I know it's only day one, but opening my eyes and looking over at Gabe, I must admit that I'm a little bit jealous of him. He has already gone a beautiful golden color and I'm a bit pink, nothing more. Hopefully I get a tan by the end of our time here.

Gabe opens one eye and catches me looking at him.

"Feel free to touch," he grins.

I laugh and slap him gently on the arm. He has no idea how much I want to touch him. After last night when he made me come harder than I have ever come in my life, I've finally allowed myself to admit that I'm starting to think of him as more than just a friend.

"Shut up," I say with a laugh. "I was just wondering why you're tanned and I'm just this pink color."

"You have plenty of time to catch up," Gabe says. He sits up. "But I reckon that's probably enough sun for one day. Are you ready to hit the spa?"

I sit up too and nod. We had debated going to the spa this morning, both of us wanting a massage and a dip in the hot tub, but when we got there, we were told we'd need to book an appointment for the massages which we've done for later in the week. We then noticed that the spa is open until eleven pm, so we decided to make the most of the sun and go down and enjoy the hot tub later on this evening.

I follow Gabe back into the suite and close the sliding door behind me.

"What do you think we'll need?" I ask.

"Nothing really," he says. "You're already wearing a bikini and the spa provides robes, towels and toiletries."

I nod and go through to the bedroom where I slip on a sundress over the top of my bikini. I debate taking under-wear for after the hot tub when my bikini will be wet, but I decide against it. It's not like I'll be going anywhere but back

up to our room. Even if we decide to go out to some of the
local bars we'll come back up here first to change. When I
come back out of the bedroom, Gabe was in the other one
and put on a pair of shorts and a t-shirt.

"Ready?" I ask him.

He nods and picks up the key card for the room and we
head out. We make our way to the elevator – we're on the
top floor, there's no way I'm walking down that many flights
of stairs – and then walk across the lobby and down the
hallway to the spa.

We arrive at the spa and the immaculate looking receptionist behind the immaculate looking desk smiles at us,
showing straight white teeth. I'm starting to feel like I'm not
the sort of person who comes to this sort of place, but Gabe
doesn't seem to notice that everything is so pristine and
perfect or if he does notice, he doesn't care. He smiles at the
woman and approaches the desk.

"Hi. Do you have appointments?" the receptionist says as
Gabe reaches the desk.

"No, but we only wanted to use the hot tub," he replies.

"Oh, that's fine," she smiles. "The hot tub and the pools
are both available and unless we have a sudden rush, you'll
have them pretty much to yourself."

She reaches below the counter and comes up with two
branded gift bags and holds them out to Gabe who takes
them.

"You'll find a towel, a robe and some toiletries in here,"
she says. "If you need anything else, don't hesitate to let me
know. Enjoy your time with us."

Gabe thanks her and I smile at her as we pass. When we
reach the changing rooms, he hands me one of the bags.

"See you on the other side," he jokes.

I laugh and then I go into the changing room. I find the lockers and take my robe out of my bag. I put the bag into the locker followed by my shoes and then my sundress. I slip into the robe and lock the locker and drop the key into the robe's pocket.

I head for the exit, running my fingers over the robe and snuggling into it. It's far from cold here but the robe is so snuggly and soft I can't resist it. I head out of the changing room and follow the signs for the pool. I know I'm getting closer as the chlorine smell gets stronger. I find the door marked pool and push it open and step through it.

A huge pool greets me and beside it, tucked away in an alcove is a hot tub that could easily hold ten people comfortably. The receptionist wasn't wrong when she told us how quiet it is. One lone man is swimming lengths in the pool and other than him, the place is empty. Even Gabe isn't here yet.

I go to the hot tub and slip out of my robe. I step in and sit down, enjoying the heat of the water and the deliciousness of the bubbles against my skin. I lean back and close my eyes, relaxing.

"Mind if I join you?" Gabe asks a couple of minutes later.

I open my eyes and smile up at him as he gets in beside me. He moans with pleasure as he gets comfortable.

"Oh, that's amazing," he says.

I nod my agreement. The only thing missing is a glass of ice-cold champagne and something tells me if I were to tell the receptionist that, that a glass would most likely appear.

After a moment, I feel Gabe's fingers on my inner thigh. His touch feels amazing, and I let myself enjoy it. His fingers start to move higher and before I know it, he has pushed my bikini bottoms to one side and his fingers have found my clit. I want nothing more than to shut my eyes and enjoy the pleasure he is bringing me, but I'm aware of us not being entirely alone.

Still, I don't immediately stop him. His touch feels too good for that, and I let him massage my clit. His insistent touch, the warmth of the water, the bubbles on my skin, it all adds up and it doesn't take long until I'm on the verge of climaxing. I know I can't let that happen when we aren't alone though, and I force myself to speak.

"Stop it," I whisper to Gabe. He stops rubbing my clit, but his fingers don't go far, resting on my inner thigh once more.

"I thought maybe you'd like a rerun of last night," Gabe whispers in my ear.

His breath tickles my neck and makes goosebumps run down my back. God, I want him so badly.

"I mean I would," I agree. "But there's someone in the pool."

"Not anymore there isn't," Gabe replies.

He pushes himself off the ledge and moves into the center of the hot tub, giving me a clear view of the now empty pool. This changes things slightly and a shiver of anticipation goes through me. Gabe moves towards me and puts his hands on my knees. He smiles at me and then in one movement, he ducks beneath the water and pushes my knees apart.

I feel a slight pressure on my lips and then they are parted, and Gabe's tongue is on my clit, licking me. I'm still close to coming from his touch and I know I won't have long to wait now that he's licking me. I also know that despite the fact that we are alone, we're still in public, and I know I'll have to be quiet when I come.

Gabe's tongue moves faster and harder and I bite down

on my lip to stop myself from crying out. My hands clench into fists on the ledge beside me and pleasure floods my body, taking my breath away.

I feel Gabe shift slightly, his tongue starting to move away from my clit. I'm too close to orgasm to let him stop now and I clench my thighs, holding his head in place against me. He seems to understand my urgency or maybe he just needs oxygen more than I thought because he is licking me with an almost ferocious intensity now and my orgasm slams through me. Pleasure floods my body, setting my nerve endings on fire and making my whole body tingle. I can feel my clit pulsing, my stomach clenching with it. I feel as though I'm just a giant ball of pleasure and it takes everything I have not to cry out.

For a second, my thighs grip Gabe's head tighter as my body goes rigid and then I force myself to relax, freeing him. He breaks the surface, and we hold each other's gaze as we both gasp for air. He looks so hot with water beaded in his hair, his body slick and slippery and my clit pulses again at the sight of him. I'm more than ready for another orgasm.

Gabe smiles at me and comes to sit next to me again. He puts his arm around me, and I lean into him, putting my head on his shoulder. A splashing sound gets our attention and we both look over at the pool. The surface breaks and the man from before surfaces and starts swimming.

Gabe and I look at each other in amused horror.

"Was he there... before?" I ask.

"I have no idea," Gabe admits.

We giggle and I can't believe that there's a possibility that I have just climaxed with a stranger in the room.

"Oh my God," I whisper, still giggling. "We have to get out of here."

"You go on ahead, I won't be far behind you," Gabe says.

I frown, confused as to why he doesn't want to get out now. He nods down into his lap. "Let's just say if I get out now, there will be no doubt about what just happened."

Realization of what he's talking about dawns on me.

"Ohhh," I say. "Well do you want me to wait?"

"No," Gabe replies. "I think I have a much better chance of it going down if you're not in the area."

I laugh at that, and Gabe laughs too, but I know he's serious and I get what he means. I'm just glad that when I get aroused by being in his presence, no one would know just by looking at me.

I turn and rub my lips lightly across Gabe's lips before I stand up.

"Ok, I'll go get dressed. Don't be too long, ok?" I ask.

"Well, you're not exactly helping me with that are you," Gabe laughs.

I grab my robe and head back to the changing rooms. I go to my locker and get the bag out again. I empty it to find a nice, soft towel, a shower gel, a shampoo, a conditioner and a small tube of lotion. It's all designer brands and it all smells amazing. I can hardly wait to get in the shower and use it all.

I slip my wet bikini off and put it in my locker and get into my robe again. I take my bits and bobs to the shower area, choose a cubicle, and get in. I hang my robe on the hook on the back of the door and then I stand underneath the warm water and shampoo my hair. I rinse the shampoo out and then I condition it and rinse it again. I slather myself in shower gel and as I rub my body my mind goes back to the orgasm I've just had, and I can't stop myself from smiling.

As I wash between my legs, I can feel that I'm still sensitive after my orgasm but despite that, I'm already craving Gabe's touch down there once more. He seems to know my body instinctively and he makes me feel pleasure like no one has ever done before. I mean don't get me wrong, I've had orgasms before obviously, but not like this. Not the kind of orgasms that I can feel in my whole body and that keep me wanting more for hours after them.

I feel like the orgasms Gabe gives me work in two ways; they satisfy a need and yet at the same time, they create an even greater need for the next one.

I shake my head, trying to shake away the thoughts of Gabe and orgasms before I get carried away. It's not easy, but I manage to focus on getting rinsed off and out of the shower. I go back to my locker area and sit down on a bench where I rub the body lotion into my skin. I pull my sundress on and pack my stuff away in the bag it all came in, adding my wet bikini last. I slip my shoes back on and go over to the sink area where I use a hair dryer on my hair. When it's dry, I realize I didn't bring a brush and I run my fingers through it until it's in some sort of a half decent state and then I exit the changing room.

I find Gabe already waiting for me and he stands up and holds his hand out and I slip my hand into his. My skin tingles where his palm touches mine and I feel a shiver of desire go through me. My clit starts to pulse, and I'm conscious of the fact that I have no underwear on, a little secret that keeps me turned on all the way back to our room.

"Should we go out onto the balcony and get some fresh air?" Gabe says.

I nod and we dump our bags and go out onto the balcony. Gabe sits down on his lounger, and I start to make for mine, but then I have a better idea. I move to the edge of the balcony and stand with my arms on the wall looking out at the sea.

Well aware of how short my dress is and that I still haven't bothered to put any panties on, I lean forward slightly and shuffle my feet backwards, knowing that Gabe is getting a view of my naked pussy and ass.

18

GABE

I sit on the lounger on our balcony and look at Clarissa where she stands with her elbows on the balcony wall looking out over the beachy area in front of the hotel. The slight breeze moves her hair back from her face a tiny bit. My eyes go to her bare legs, legs that she thinks are pink but are already turning brown. She has amazing legs, long, slender, and shapely. My gaze roams up her legs and stops at the hem of her dress where it sits mid-thigh. I know what's beneath that dress and already I want to taste her again. I want to push my fingers into her and then my cock, fill her up and make her scream my name.

I can feel myself getting hard as I think about how good Clarissa's pussy would feel wrapped around my cock. I can't take my eyes off her sexy ass and hips, even when she starts to move. She takes a small step back, but she keeps her elbows where they are, and her dress rides up.

My breath catches in my throat when I see her ass and pussy bare beneath her dress, no panties in sight. My jaw has dropped, and I'm staring at her glistening slit, unable to look away. I'm wondering if she is doing this on purpose, a way to get my attention and let me know she wants me to fill her up, or if she just innocently moved and has no idea that I can see her pussy.

When that thought occurs to me, I force myself to tear my eyes away from the delicious sight. I suddenly feel like a pervert watching her this way when she might not be aware of it.

I swallow and my throat makes a dry clicking sound. I could use a glass of water, but I ignore the thirst, more interested in the other thing I'm thirsting for. I want to ask Clarissa if she is teasing me on purpose, if she wants me to come to her, but I can't find the right words to ask the question. How do you ask someone if they're flashing you on purpose or not without embarrassing the hell out of them if they're not doing it on purpose?

A couple of seconds that feel like a couple of hours pass. I still don't dare to look at Clarissa but I'm still very much aware of her naked pussy close enough to touch if I reach out. Clarissa looks at me over her shoulder and she gives me this sexy smile and I know then that she knows exactly what she's doing and that her display is indeed for my benefit.

"What are you waiting for? A handwritten invitation?" she purrs.

Her voice is low and thick with lust and hearing her speak like that is enough to almost send me over the edge. I'm on my feet practically before she's finished her sentence. I go to her and hold my hand out to her, but she shakes her head and grins.

"Here," she says.

I raise an eyebrow, but I'm not about to deny her if that's what she wants. I move behind her and run my hands up the backs of her legs and up over her ass cheeks. I move them around her hips and over her stomach and then back again. Keeping one hand on her hip, I push my fingers inside of her and begin to move them in and out, slowly at first and then faster when Clarissa moans.

She moves her hips in time with my fingers, pulling them deeper into her and making sure the friction of them rubs over her g-spot. I take my other hand off her hip and move it around to the front of her body where I push my fingers between her lips. I massage her clit in time with my thrusting fingers.

I work her until I know she is on the very edge of coming and then I stop, pulling my hands away from her. I smile to myself when she moans in frustration.

"God Gabe, don't stop, please," she says, her voice low and husky.

I feel a pulse of desire flood through me as I push my shorts down and step out of them. I take my hard cock in my hand and run it between her ass cheeks and down past her pussy and through her lips, spreading her wetness around. She moans again as I bring it back and when I plunge into her, she makes an 'ahh' sound that is music to my ears.

Her pussy is wet, hot and tight, exactly as I had imagined it would be. It envelops me and seems to pull me in deeper. I push into her until she takes my full length and then I pull almost all the way back out before filling her again. My moan joins hers as we move together.

I move my hands beneath her dress as we move together and run them over her stomach and up to her chest. I cup her breasts in my hands, kneading them and rubbing her nipples. Her nipples harden at my touch, and I roll them between my thumb and forefinger. Clarissa moans again and I reward her with an extra hard thrust that makes her gasp.

I move my hands from her breasts. One hand moves to

her back and my fingers lightly trace her spine from the top to the bottom and then I move my hand across her ass cheek and rest it on her hip. My other hand stays at the front of her body. I move it down her stomach and over her pubic bone and then I once again find her clit with my fingers. She cries out as I begin to work her clit in time with my thrusts.

I know the moment her orgasm hits her. Her body goes rigid, and her pussy tightens around me. I feel a gush of warm liquid coating me and I feel her clit throbbing. I move my hands to her hips and use them to keep her moving in time to my thrusts.

She cries out and then makes a low moaning sound and then her rigidity softens once more, and I figure she is coasting back down right now. Her knees buckle and it's only because of my hands on her hips that she doesn't fall to the ground. I keep my grip on her hips, keeping her up and moving her in time with my thrusting.

My own orgasm is seconds away now and when Clarissa clenches around me, I know I can't hold myself back any longer. I relax and let my orgasm wash over me. I hold Clarissa's hips, holding her in place with my cock fully inside of her and her ass pressing up against my lower stomach.

My climax slams through my body, the pleasure starting in my cock and then filtering up into my stomach and then radiating out across my whole body. I try to suck in a breath, but I find that I can't do it. My throat works but no air gets in. My lungs start to burn but I barely notice that sensation for the tingling, amazing feeling that's spreading through me.

Finally, when I don't think I can take it any longer, my climax begins to recede, and I can breathe again. I take in a deep, shuddering breath. It sears my throat, but it brings a pleasant relief with it despite the pain and I'm soon panting and gasping, trying to get myself under control. My legs are shaking, and I don't think I can hold both myself and Clarissa up for much longer.

I put my hands on Clarissa's stomach and pull her upper body up against me and then I move backwards with her in my arms until my legs hit the lounger behind me. I turn around and lay Clarissa down on her side on the lounger and then I get on it beside her. We wrap our arms around each other, and I kiss Clarissa on the lips.

"Wow," she says after we end our kiss. "We are most definitely doing that again."

"Give me a minute to recover from that and then I'm all yours," I smile.

Clarissa kisses me and without taking her lips from mine, she shuffles around so that she's on her knees straddling me. When she has herself in position, she breaks her lips from mine and smiles down at me.

"Or we could just go again right now," she whispers.

19

CLARISSA

I look down at Gabe and I can see the desire on his face. I smile and move my hips, rubbing my pussy over his cock. I feel him hardening beneath me and I know he's more than ready to go again. I take the bottom of his t-shirt and he lifts himself enough that I can drag it up and over his head. I drop it on the ground and then I pull my dress off, dropping it onto the pile.

I love how the breeze feels caressing my bare skin and I love the contrast between the cool night air and the heat from Gabe's body. My nipples are hardening as the cold air wraps itself around them and I can't help but reach up and play with them. Gabe makes an 'mmm' sound as I play with my nipples, a sound that makes me want to ride him all night long.

Gabe grabs my wrists, pulling my fingers away from my nipples while pulling me down towards him. He maneuvers me around so that my nipple ends up in his mouth. The warmth of his mouth and the roughness of his tongue on my nipple makes me moan. The feeling moves down through my body to my pussy and I feel it clench as my body screams for more and I need to feel Gabe inside of me once more.

I don't make myself wait any longer. I pull myself back up into a sitting position and I reach down behind me and grab Gabe's cock in my hand. I hold it still and push myself down on it. I move my hand away and keep lowering myself until I've taken Gabe's full length inside of me. I can feel how full I am, how stretched my pussy is and I love it.

I start to move, lifting my body up and then down slowly, savoring every second of our bodies moving together. My pussy is tender from the battering it has already taken but it's a good tender, a stinging sensation that mixes with the pleasure and makes it a whole new but no less enjoyable experience.

Gabe bucks his hips, trying to make me move faster but I don't want to move faster; I want to tease him, to make him crazy with the need for me. He puts his hands on my hips, trying to move me faster. I take his hands in mine and move them gently away from my hips and then I keep moving at my slow, agonizing pace.

I feel every little part of Gabe's cock slither over me, and I can feel a constant pulsing need deep down inside of me. I know I can't hold myself back for much longer and I start to move faster. I release Gabe's hands and he doesn't disappoint me, his hands going straight to my hips and helping me to lift myself up and down faster and faster.

Gabe is thrusting in time with me now and I feel like I'm about to explode as my body bounces up and down, my breasts jiggling wildly. I know I could climax right now if I let myself go, but I want to hold myself off until Gabe comes so that we can share our orgasm. It's not going to be easy, not when I'm this filled with pleasure and lust, but I have to try. I watch Gabe's face as I move on top of him, looking for any clues that he's almost there with me.

Just when I think I'm not going to be able to hold myself back for much longer, Gabe's face begins to change, his mouth twisting, contorting with his nearing orgasm. I move faster and I clench my pussy, tightening myself around Gabe's cock. I hear him gasp and I see his mouth drop open and I know he's now right on the edge. I clench tightly around his cock again and as I do it, I let go of my self-control and let my climax take me.

My orgasm slams through me, starting in my clit and lower stomach, making my pussy clench again and then spreading through my whole body, transporting me to a place where only pleasure matters. I feel Gabe spurt inside of me and I clench again as he moans my name.

He thrusts once more, taking me by surprise and hitting my g-spot, making my orgasm draw on for longer until I think I can't take the intensity of the feeling any longer. Finally, the feeling starts to fade leaving me feeling so content and happy. Gabe slips out of me, and we shuffle around until we're back laying side by side in each other's arms, our noses almost touching. We kiss, a gentle, tender kiss and then Gabe rolls onto his back, keeping his arm wrapped tightly around my shoulders.

I snuggle up against Gabe, resting my cheek on his chest and putting my palm flat on his stomach. It's nice just to lay there in his arms, my swollen clit reminding me of the fun we just had. I can hear the sea lapping gently on the beach and I can smell the salt in the air. If this isn't paradise, then I don't know what is.

After a few minutes, I start to feel my eyes closing and I know if I don't move soon, I'm going to end up falling asleep.

"Should we go inside?" I ask.

Gabe's grip on me tightens.

"In a little bit," he says.

His voice is thick and slurred and I realize he was already asleep. His grip on me loosens slightly as he drifts back off to sleep. I should probably wake him but it's not like it's cold here and it's so nice just lying in his arms. I decide to give it half an hour or so and then wake him and insist we go inside.

I WAKE up laid on my side, the heat of the sun drifting over me. I yawn and stretch and go to sit up and then panic grips me when I realize I'm naked. What the fuck. It only takes a second for my memory of last night to come back and for me to realize that I haven't just drifted off to sleep on the beach.

I do sit up now, and I smile sleepily when I see Gabe perched on the end of the other lounger watching me. He's sipping from a mug with steam coming out of it and he picks another mug up and hands it to me. I thank him gratefully and bring the mug up to my face, inhaling the delicious coffee smell off the steam. I take a sip and moan in pleasure at the taste. I drink a little bit more.

"Did you go off to bed in the night and leave me out here on my own?" I ask.

Gabe laughs and shakes his head.

"No. I woke up about half an hour ago. I went and had a shower and then went down to the restaurant to grab us some coffees," he says. "You're lucky you woke up when you did, or I might have had to drink yours too."

"That would have been a low blow," I laugh.

"All's fair in love and coffee," Gabe replies with a grin.

We drink our coffee looking out towards the ocean, each of us lost in our own thoughts. I don't know what Gabe is thinking about, but I have a feeling it's the same thing I'm thinking about – last night. I just hope he's thinking along the same lines as I am.

I loved last night. It was amazing and not just because it was by far the best sex I've ever had. I felt a real emotional connection with Gabe, and I know if I let myself, I could fall completely, head over heels in love with him. But as much as I want to let myself love him; I can't do it. Not yet. Every time I tell myself I'm over Michael and what he did to me, I can't help but imagine how I would feel if Gabe cheated on me.

I find myself picturing him with other women when that happens, and it makes me feel sick to my core. I can't risk it. Not yet. I'm just not ready. I don't want to turn into some jealous nag that gets insecure every time my man speaks to another woman, but I really think that's how I would be if we got into a relationship right now. I don't need that kind of energy in my life and Gabe doesn't deserve to be painted as the bad guy when he's done nothing wrong. He deserves to be with someone who can trust him.

I know I have to tell Gabe how I'm feeling but I really don't want to hurt him and I don't want the rest of our honeymoon to be awkward. It would be wrong to keep these feelings to myself until after the honeymoon though. It would just feel like I was leading Gabe on.

"Can we talk?" I say, cutting through the peaceful silence that hung between us.

"Of course," Gabe says. "What's up?"

"I... I..." I stop and take a breath and start over again. "Last night was amazing. It was everything I could have wanted and more. But it can't happen again. As much as I want it to, I'm just not ready for a relationship right now and I don't want to get myself all tangled up in a messy situation and then end up losing my best friend."

"You don't want to lose me, yet you feel it's appropriate to dump me on our honeymoon?" Gabe says.

I feel shocked. I don't know what reaction I was expecting, but it wasn't this. I open my mouth to tell him it's not like that, but he starts to laugh and shakes his head.

"I'm joking Clarissa," he says. "I'm sorry. It was in bad taste, but I just wanted to lighten the mood a bit."

"Oh," I say. Again, he's caught me on the back foot and left me unsure of what to say next. "So, no hard feelings then?"

"None at all," Gabe says. "I'm sorry. I shouldn't have let anything happen between us."

"Oh no, don't be sorry," I say. "I'm glad it happened. I don't regret it at all. I just don't want to rush into anything more, that's all."

Gabe smiles at me, a look of amusement on his face.

"Ok Clarissa whatever you say," he tells me, the smile still on his face.

"I'm serious Gabe," I say.

"I believe you," he says, still half laughing. "But I think it would be easier for me to think you meant this if you weren't sitting there naked."

I feel heat rush to my cheeks. I had completely forgotten that I was naked and I'm not surprised Gabe was laughing when I was trying to have a serious conversation like that with him with no clothes on.

Gabe throws me my sundress from the balcony floor. I shake it to get any loose sand off it and I slip it on. I stand up and quickly pull it down and then I sit back down.

"There," I say. "Now do I look like I mean it?"

Gabe nods his head and stands up.

"You do," he says. "I'm just going to head inside a moment."

I don't know if he's upset or if he wants to use the bathroom or something and just doesn't want to say anything. I really don't want things between us to be awkward, but I can't just demand things and then expect Gabe to not feel his feelings.

I become aware of a shadow falling over me as Gabe passes behind me. The shadow doesn't move though, and I realize Gabe has stopped walking. I feel the lounger move slightly as Gabe gets on it behind me. I feel his warm lips on my neck and then they move along my collar bone, kissing and licking and making me moan in desire. His mouth moves off my skin, but it stays close enough that when he speaks, his breath tickles my skin.

"Are you sure you don't want to do this anymore?" he asks, before lightly kissing my neck again.

I can't help but move my head to the side, giving him easier access to my neck. He doesn't disappoint, running his tongue down my neck and then back up again, sending shivers through my body. I know I should stop this, but I don't think I can.

No, I have to. He's never going to believe I'm serious about us only being friends if I melt this way at his every touch.

"Gabe please," I say. "Don't make this harder than it has to be. I'm really not ready for a relationship. I wish I was, but I'm not."

"Who said anything about a relationship?" Gabe says. "You said it yourself. The sex last night was amazing. Let's do that again, just as a casual thing."

"I... I don't know. I'm scared one of us will get attached and end up getting hurt," I say.

"Ok, I'll make you a deal," Gabe says. "While we're on our honeymoon, we'll keep up appearances and act like newlyweds who are desperately in love. Which of course means lots of hot sex. Then when we go home, we go back to reality. Unless you change your mind. In which case, you can just let me know."

Now he's got my attention. That could actually work, and it might give us a chance to get each other out of our systems too. I nod slowly and then I smile.

"It would be awfully rude to be on our honeymoon and not act like we're on a real honeymoon wouldn't it," I say.

"Exactly. And we don't want to be rude now do we?" he says.

"Nope, definitely not," I say with a smile.

Gabe wraps his arms around me, and I turn within his arms to face him. Our lips touch and even as I tell myself it's just an arrangement, it's not real, we will be normal when we get home again, I can already tell I'm in big trouble here.

20

─────

GABE

We've been back from our honeymoon for eleven days now. Clarissa has given up her apartment and moved into mine. It's been great living with her, although I do wish we could be more than just roommates. I would give anything to hold her in my arms as we fall asleep and to wake up with her beside me each morning. But true to her word, she hasn't let me know that she's changed her mind about our relationship being anything more than just platonic.

I don't mind in one sense. I love having her around and I would rather have this with her than nothing. I will happily forego any future relationships to have Clarissa in my life. And of course, I can keep on hoping that she will change her mind in time. At no point has she actually come out and said that she doesn't want a relationship with me specifically. It's always been that she's not ready for a relationship in general. I am still hopeful that one day, she will be ready to love again and when that day comes, I can only hope that she chooses me to take a leap of faith with. And if she doesn't, well I get to live out my days with my best friend and that will be enough for me. It's more than a lot of people get to do so I suppose in that sense, I am lucky.

The best part about it all is that I think Clarissa is truly happy here too. I no longer catch her looking sad when she thinks no one is watching. And she barely mentions her ex and his betrayal now. I'm not saying she's over him, but she's certainly acting like she's found a way to be happy despite what he did to her. We often sit up late just talking and our conversations mention her ex and her broken heart less and less. We mostly talk about the future now with the baby or we just chat general shit and make each other laugh.

I feel closer to Clarissa than I ever have before, even before she left for Europe. I think some of that is an age thing; our friendship has stood the test of time and the test of long distance, and I think being back together after all of those years apart and just falling back into our routines has shown us both that we truly are best friends for life. I also think that having Clarissa live with me has brought us closer. They say you don't truly know a person until you live with them.

I don't know if that's strictly true or not, but I do feel a lot closer to Clarissa since she moved in here and I think she would say the same thing about me too.

I'm distracted from my thoughts when Clarissa comes out of her bedroom and rushes into the living room where I'm sitting. She's half hopping and half running, bent double as she tries to pull on her shoe without stopping.

"What's wrong?" I ask. "Why are you rushing around like a maniac?"

"I'm supposed to be at work in five minutes," Clarissa says. "I fell asleep after my shower and now I'm going to be so late."

I shrug my shoulders and smile at her.

"Yeah, I'm pretty sure your boss isn't going to be too worried about it," I say.

"No, it's not you I'm worried about," Clarissa says. "It's the others. I don't want to be that guy. You know the one who marries her boss and thinks she's above everyone else and can do what she likes? I don't care what people think of me generally, but I hate that guy myself and I refuse to become someone who thinks it's ok to act like that."

As she talks, she finally gets her foot settled in her shoe and she grabs her purse from the table. She heads for the door.

"See you later," she says.

I jump up and grab my keys off the table in front of me.

"I have to pop into the bar at some point today to check on all the orders and inventory. Might as well make it now and I can give you a ride and save you jogging there," I say.

"Thank you, that'll be great," she says.

We hurry down to the car and I drive us straight to the bar. As I pull up, I note the time. Clarissa is only two or three minutes late. I've barely stopped the car and her door is open and she's running towards the bar. I can't help but laugh to myself watching her.

She's so cute when she's flustered like this. I get out of the car, lock it, and follow Clarissa into the bar. She's already behind the bar, her cheeks flushed and her hair a bit fly away from rushing. Even from here I can hear her apologizing to Penny.

Penny waves her apology away telling her not to worry, she was barely even late. I know Penny would have said the same thing if we weren't now married. She's a fair boss and she gets it that sometimes, life happens, and people can run a minute or two late. She wouldn't make a big deal out of it unless it became a regular thing.

I go behind the bar myself and greet Penny. I beckon to her to follow me as I go through the door to the back part of the bar where my office, the staff break room and the staff bathrooms are.

"Anything I need to know?" I ask.

Penny shakes her head.

"No, everything is fine," she says. "Oh, but Peter from the brewery did call. He said it was just a courtesy call, but you might want to call him back."

I nod. I'm about to thank Penny and walk away when she puts her fingers to her lips and seems to be listening. I listen as well, and I hear Rebecca's voice coming from the bar area.

"Nice of you to finally join us," she says.

I know she's having a go at Clarissa, and I bristle. I want to go out there and tell Rebecca to fuck off and not bother coming back, but I know Clarissa can handle herself and Penny sorts the staff out. I don't want to go over her head and start firing people unless there's something major that happens.

"I'm sorry," Clarissa says. "I fell asleep and when I woke up it was almost time for me to be here."

"Fell asleep," Rebecca sneers. "That's no excuse. Have you never heard of an alarm clock?"

"Well of course I have but it's not like I was planning on going to sleep. What do you think I should do? Just randomly set alarms for regular times throughout the day just in case?" Clarissa fires back.

"Well, if it would get you to work on time, then yes," Rebecca says.

It seems that Penny has heard enough because she steps away from me and back into the bar area.

"That's enough Rebecca," she says. "You're not the

manager here and it's not your place to be chastising other members of staff."

"Sorry," Rebecca mutters, sounding anything but sorry.

I smile to myself, imagining Clarissa's face at Rebecca's mumbled apology. I debate going out there and saying something myself, but Penny has it handled and if I interrupt her now it will make her authority look weak. Instead, I go to my office.

I sit down and quickly call Peter back. Penny was right about it being a courtesy call; he just wants to make sure we're happy with everything and I tell him that we are. After the call, I fire up my computer and check my emails and then I update the books with some receipts I needed to record.

I leave the office and go down to the cellar where I make a note of what stock we have left and what I need to order. I go back upstairs ready to call in and place my order. I open my office door and jump when I see Rebecca standing there in the middle of my office. I had no idea she was there, and it wasn't like I was expecting someone to be standing there.

"Sorry," Rebecca says with a smile when I jump.

"It's ok," I tell her. "What's up? Does Penny need me for something?"

"No. Actually there was something I wanted to talk to you about," she says.

I perch on the edge of my desk and nod towards the chair facing me. Rebecca smiles and heads for the chair. She pauses as she moves towards it, her head on one side looking at me.

"You look different," she says. "Have you had a haircut?"

I shake my head. I probably look different because I'm living with the woman of my dreams, even if we're not officially together. I know Rebecca has a bit of a crush on me, and while I certainly don't feel the same way about her, I don't want to hurt her for the sake of it and so I don't tell her my theory on why I look different, I just shake my head in answer to her question.

She moves closer to me and puts her hand on my chest. She smiles at me.

"You've been working out, haven't you? That's what it is," she says.

I move backwards quickly, pulling away from her touch without consciously thinking about it. She pouts at me, looking sad, but I draw the line at letting her touch me to keep her happy. Apart from anything, it would only be leading her on.

"I haven't been working out either. Now please keep your hands to yourself and tell me what you actually want," I say.

"Ooh there's no need to be so touchy jeez. I was just giving you a compliment," Rebecca says as she sits down in the chair I gestured to what feels like an hour ago. I don't respond to that; I just keep looking at her questioningly waiting to find out what she wants. "I really need next Friday off."

"Ok," I say, surprised she's bringing this to me. "Well, you'll need to talk to Penny. You know she handles all that sort of stuff."

"I've already asked Penny about it, but she said no," Rebecca says.

"So, what makes you think I will go over her head?" I ask, getting a little bit annoyed by this whole conversation now.

Rebecca looks down into her lap for a second and when she looks back up at me, her eyes shine with unshed tears.

"I... I found a lump in my breast. I have to go to the hospital to have tests done," Rebecca says.

"And Penny said no to you having the day off for that?" I say with a frown, sure I must have misunderstood her.

"I didn't tell her why I needed it off," Rebecca says. That makes more sense. There's no way Penny would have said no to such a request. "I didn't feel comfortable discussing something so personal with Penny."

I reach out and lightly squeeze her shoulder.

"Don't worry, I'll take care of it," I say. "I hope everything goes well for you."

"Thank you," she says.

She stands up and steps towards me with her arms outstretched. I assume she wants a hug because she still looks teary eyed and for all my instincts scream at me not to do this, the poor girl must be terrified after what she's just told me. How can I just push her away after that?

I open my arms and Rebecca steps into them. She rests her head on my shoulder and I let her stay there for a moment before I clear my throat and let her know this is getting uncomfortable. She seems to take the hint as she lifts her head up. I'm horrified though when I see her eyes are closed and her lips are parted and she's moving in for a kiss.

I take my arms from around her and grab her upper arms lightly. I don't want to hurt her; I just want to stop her from kissing me.

"Rebecca, no," I say. "We can only ever be friends."

"I know," she says, taking a small step back. "I got carried away there. Sorry." Before I can say anything else she goes back to talking about the hospital and I instantly feel bad and decide against saying anything else to her. "So, I can definitely have Friday off then to keep my appointment."

"Yes, of course," I say. "And if you need any further time to get your results or whatever just let me know, ok?"

"I will. Thank you for being so understanding," she says.

"Of course," I tell her.

21

GABE

I'm starting to feel hungry, and I decide to go and see if Clarissa is due her break and see if she wants to go and grab something to eat. I go through the bar door, but I don't see Clarissa behind the bar and a quick scan of the room tells me she's not out there waitressing or collecting the empty glasses. Penny must have her doing something on the upstairs bar. I go towards the stairs, but I see another bartender, Zac, already heading up that way.

"If you see Clarissa up there, can you let her know I want her for something please?" I ask.

"She just went on her break," Zac says. "I saw her go out. Is there anything I can do for you?"

"No, it's fine, it wasn't a work thing. Thanks though," I tell him.

I head for the door and step out into the street wondering where Clarissa might have gone. There's really only one place I can think of that will be open now other than a fancy restaurant and that's the diner over on the next block. I start heading for it.

I'm not some crazy stalker type and normally I wouldn't

dream of doing this, but it strikes me as odd that Clarissa would go off on her break without coming to see if I was joining her like she has every break she's had since we got back off our honeymoon. If I have upset her somehow, I would much rather she just come to me than play games, especially in front of my staff.

I reach the diner and peer in through the window. Sure enough, I see Clarissa sitting there looking down at her table. She's poking at a salad with a fork, but she doesn't seem to be eating it, rather she's just playing with it.

I go inside and go to the counter where I grab a ham and cheese sandwich and a bottle of coke and then I head towards Clarissa's table. I'm practically sitting down before she looks up from her plate. She doesn't smile or say hello when she sees me, she just goes back to poking at her salad. I sit down and take a bite of my sandwich. I chew and swallow it and still Clarissa hasn't spoken to me.

"Do you want to talk about it?" I ask.

"Talk about what?" she says.

"Whatever it is that I'm supposed to have done to have you stop speaking to me," I say.

I keep working on my sandwich. Clarissa spears a slice of cucumber on her fork, and she finally brings it to her mouth. She looks at me thoughtfully as she chews it.

"What do you think you've done?" she asks.

"I have no idea and I don't have the time or the energy to play mind games Clarissa," I say. "Please either tell me what has happened or let it go."

"Do you remember when we first talked about this marriage? We came up with three rules. Can you remember what they are?" she asks.

"Sure," I say. "Separate bedrooms, no cheating, and I'm to tell you if I want out."

"Right," she says. "And when did we discuss any of those rules no longer being in play?"

"We didn't," I say.

"Right," Clarissa says again. "So, forgive me if I'm being naïve but if we haven't discussed changing the rules, then they haven't changed. Right?"

"Right," I say.

"So, you know what you've done then," she says.

"Nope. I don't have a clue what I'm meant to have done," I say. "Unless I sleepwalked last night and ended up in your room, in which case, I'm sorry."

Normally she would have laughed at that but this time, she just shakes her head and looks away from me.

"Ok I'm sorry. I shouldn't have tried to make a joke out of the situation. But honestly, I have no idea what I've done to upset you," I say.

She spears another slice of cucumber and nibbles on it, leaving it on the fork and taking tiny bites while, I assume, she contemplates what she is going to tell me.

"I saw you Gabe," she says after a moment. That doesn't help me one little bit and so I just stay quiet and hope she will go on. She does. "With her. Rebecca. You touched her shoulder and then you held her and kissed her."

It takes everything I have not to choke on the half-chewed bite of sandwich that's in my mouth. I swallow it quickly while I shake my head.

"I can assure you that I didn't kiss Rebecca," I say.

"Right," Clarissa says in a tone of voice that says she doesn't believe that for a second. "But you admit to the rest?"

I'm torn with what I'm supposed to say. Of course, I want to explain to Clarissa what happened, and she is my wife; she deserves an explanation to some extent. But at the same time, employee confidentiality is a big thing, and I don't think it's right that we should be discussing Rebecca's health concerns. I try to think of how to phrase it well enough to appease Clarissa without telling her Rebecca's business.

"Well? Cat got your tongue, has it?" Clarissa says with a frown. "I think your silence says it all."

I'm going to have to just tell her the bare bones of Rebecca's issues and if she pushes me, I'll tell her all of it and beg her not to say anything to anyone. Employee confidentiality is one thing, but Clarissa is far more important to me than any employment laws.

"Rebecca came to my office today. She's had some bad news and because of it, she needed to have a day off," I say. "She came to me because she wasn't comfortable discussing it with Penny. She got upset when we were talking and so yes, I gave her shoulder a little squeeze as I would with any of my staff if they were visibly upset. She came in for a hug afterwards. What was I supposed to do? Push her away?"

Clarissa is silent for a moment and then she sighs.

"Well, no, not if she was upset. But there's a difference between hugging someone because they are upset and kissing them, Gabe. That's the point you should have pushed her away," she says.

"Ah right, you mean the point I actually did push her away then," I say. "Let me guess. You saw her moving in for a kiss and turned around and flounced off before I stopped it."

"I wouldn't say flounced," Clarissa says, her cheeks reddening as she realizes that I have done nothing wrong. "More like stormed."

"Whatever. Take my advice Clarissa. If you're going to spy at my office door, then stay until the full encounter is done with, ok?" I say.

She sighs.

"I'm sorry. I shouldn't have been spying at all. I mean it

didn't start that way. I came to ask you something but then I saw Rebecca there and your hand was on her shoulder and... yeah, I shouldn't have spied. But let's not forget the major line Rebecca crossed. She knows for a fact we're married. Fuck she was at our wedding for crying out loud. And now she's trying to kiss you?" Clarissa says, her voice getting louder towards the end of her speech.

I grin and she frowns.

"You're jealous," I say.

"No, I'm not. We just have boundaries, and we need to stick to them, that's all," she says. I grin and raise one eyebrow and Clarissa sighs again. "Ok, fine. Maybe I am a little bit jealous. Is that so wrong of me?"

"Not at all," I say, stopping teasing her. I reach for her hand on the table. I cover it with mine and squeeze it. "I'll talk to her and make it clear that's not to happen again."

"And no more flirting either tell her," Clarissa says.

"Ok, that as well," I say. "So, are we good now?"

Clarissa nods her head. I finish my sandwich and Clarissa finishes her salad. I'm surprised to see her eating properly now. Does that mean she was picking at the salad, because she thought she was losing me? No, it can't be that. Can it?

"Ready?" Clarissa says after we've finished eating and sat chatting for a while. "I only have five minutes of my break left."

I nod and we stand up and leave the diner. We make the short walk back to the bar and go inside. We are barely in the door when Clarissa grabs the back of a chair with one hand. She bends forwards slightly and presses her other hand to her stomach.

"Are you ok?" I ask.

She straightens back up and nods her head.

"Yeah. I just got a pain in my stomach. I must have eaten too quickly or something," she says.

She barely finishes her sentence before she bends double again and this time, she makes a sound that's higher than a moan but not quite a scream. I put one hand on her elbow, the other on the bottom of her back.

"Come on, let's get you in the back," I say.

She nods and we start walking, me supporting Clarissa as we go. Penny comes running over as we approach.

"What are you doing? Get her to the emergency room," she says.

"Emergency room?" I ask.

"No, I'm ok," Clarissa says at the same time.

"You're bleeding," Penny says quietly.

I look down and I feel my stomach roll when I see the streaks of red blood running down Clarissa's legs. She looks down and sees them too and when she looks back up at me, her face is white, and horror stricken.

"It's ok," I tell her. "Everything is going to be ok."

I turn her around and with Penny on her other side, we get her outside and to the parking lot and into my car.

22

CLARISSA

I sit in Gabe's car staring ahead as he speeds towards the hospital. I keep getting these horrible pains in my stomach, like something inside of me is twisting tightly. I didn't realize I was bleeding until Penny pointed it out, but now I know, I can feel the wetness of the blood coming out of me anytime I move. I try my best to keep still, even taking short, shallow breaths so that my lungs don't expand too far. I convince myself that if I can just keep still until I get to the hospital, my baby will stay put and be ok.

I can feel tears hot and ticklish rolling down my face but reaching up to wipe them away is out of the question. It would be another pointless movement that could cause a disaster.

Although I'm staying still and looking forward, I'm still aware of how Gabe keeps glancing at me, and I want to tell him that I'm ok but I can't because I'm not ok. I'm not. I'm in pain and I'm afraid and I don't know what the hell to do.

"Almost there, hang in there," Gabe tells me.

He takes one hand off the wheel and rubs my knee. His touch is warm and comforting and part of me craves his touch and wants to beg him not to ever take his hand away. The other part of me panics that even the gentle touch of his caress is going to dislodge my baby. I know it's a crazy thought, but I feel crazy right now.

"You're going to be ok," Gabe says.

I know he's trying to make me feel better, but how am I going to be ok? I can feel my baby's life ebbing away every second and there's just no way I can recover from that I don't think. I don't think I will ever be ok again.

"You know sometimes bleeding doesn't mean what you think it means," he adds.

He can't even bring himself to say it. He knows I'm losing my baby but he's trying to be nice about it. I mean he's not entirely wrong. I have heard of women bleeding when pregnant and their baby being ok, but not like this. That would surely be more like spotting than blood running down their legs and the pain. That isn't the sort of pain that means nothing. But it's more than all of that. It's more than a physical feeling. It's deeper than that. More primal. I just know on an instinctive level that I'm losing my baby. I just hope we can get to the hospital quickly enough that some doctor might be able to work a miracle and save the baby.

We arrive at the hospital and Gabe parks as close to the entrance as he can. He throws open his door.

"Wait here," he says.

Like I have a choice. I don't think I could stand up now even if I wanted to. My head is spinning, and I feel nauseous. I think it might be from the loss of blood, but it could just as easily be from my anxiety about the situation.

I watch Gabe run into the entrance of the emergency room. He grabs a wheelchair, and I can't hear what he's saying but I can see his lips moving and I'm guessing he must be shouting for help. He runs back out of the hospital with the wheelchair and by the time he reaches the car, several nurses are running behind him.

He throws my door open and reaches into me. I take his arm and slowly start to swivel around on the seat. I manage to get my legs outside of the car. I feel warm wetness running from me as I move, and I try to bite back a sob, but I can't. The sound that comes from me doesn't sound human; it sounds like an animal in pain, unable to verbalize how they are feeling, knowing only that it fucking hurts.

The nurses have reached the car now and as Gabe takes one of my arms, a pretty blonde nurse takes the other. She and Gabe nod to each other and gently pull me to my feet. I scream as another pain bends me double. Gabe and the nurse get me into the wheelchair and as I sit down, I'm hit by a wave of nausea so strong I can't swallow it down. I lean over the arm of the wheelchair and throw up. I retch even once my stomach is empty of everything I've eaten or drunk in what feels like my entire life.

My head is spinning faster and faster as the nurses rush me into the hospital, straight past the waiting room and down to the treatment rooms. I'm unconscious before they get me there. As the blackness takes over my vision, I welcome the oblivion it brings, but before I slip away, I need to see Gabe. I need to know he's here, but I don't see him and panic sets in. Has he left me when I need him the most?

"Please don't let anything happen to her," I hear Gabe say and I know he is there just out of my line of sight, and I let myself float away.

I WALK into Gabe's apartment; I suppose I should say our apartment now - but for how long? – and suddenly the loss hits me in a way that it didn't in the hospital. It was hard in the hospital of course. That awful moment when the doctor told me he was sorry, but I had lost my baby. And then the tests and the obstetrician. The poking. The prodding. The swabbing. The bleeding. The pain. It was like a waking nightmare, a horrible dream that had become a reality. It was painful like nothing I had ever known.

But this pain. This pain is different. It's raw like an open wound and it hurts so fucking much I feel like I'm drowning in heart break. Coming back here and seeing the lounge where he or she would have sat in their bouncy chair and grinned their gummy little smile. The nursery where he or she would have slept. The bathroom where he or she would have taken their first bath. All of it just came rushing in as we stepped into the apartment, and it's too much for me.

I can't breathe. This pain is too heavy for me to bear. It's like an ache in my heart, a constant, throbbing ache that drums itself through my whole body. The physical pain is gone now for the most part, numbed by pills, but the mental pain is much worse and there isn't a pill in the world that can take that pain away.

It's funny in a sense because I didn't want a baby yet. Especially not Michael's baby. And it wasn't until my baby was gone that I realized not only had I grown used to the idea of becoming a mom, but I had also grown to love the unborn bean inside of me. I had gotten to the point where I wanted the baby, needed the baby. And now he or she is gone, and I'm left empty and alone.

"Are you alright?" Gabe says from behind me.

It's only when he speaks that I realize I've stopped walking. I want to start again. Or turn to face Gabe. Or even reply to him. But I can't. My body is lead and my voice has been taken away from me, ripped from my body like my baby. I just stand there mute, frozen. And then the tears come.

There is nothing dainty or lady like about the tears. It's not a single pretty little tear running down my face. This is full on ugly crying. The kind that makes you hiccup and hitch your shoulders. The kind that takes your breath away and makes your nose run and your face and chest go bright red and blotchy. The kind that paints a picture of the pain you are feeling, that takes the ugliness from the pain and shows it to the world. It's the kind of crying I would normally only do alone where no one could see me, but right now, I don't care who sees me. I just have to let it out.

My knees buckle and I drop to the ground. I stay there on my knees, and I throw my head back and scream up at the ceiling, a long scream that sears my throat. I put my hands over my face and bend double at the waist, sobbing and rocking myself.

I don't know how long I'm down there before I sense a presence beside me and then I feel gentle hands on me, hands that pull me into warm, comforting arms. I don't hug Gabe back - I can't take my hands from my face where they clench, and the nails dig into my cheeks – but his touch is comforting in a way. It reminds me that at least for now, I am not alone with this.

Time has lost all meaning. I don't know if it's been a minute, an hour, a day, when my sobs start to subside into pathetic sounding whimpers. I haven't run out of pain. My body has just run out of the energy needed to express it. My eyes feel heavy and swollen, my limbs are like lead. I don't have the energy to move from this spot. I will just curl up here and stay here forever.

Gabe shifts and his arms go away leaving me bereft once more, but the feeling doesn't last long because after a second, his arms are back, but this time, he isn't just holding me, he's lifting me. He cradles me in his arms, pressing me against his chest. He carries me down the hallway and pauses at my bedroom door. The thought of being alone is too much to bear and I shake my head. Gabe seems to understand because he moves away from the door and takes me to his bedroom.

He lays me down on his bed and I curl up into a fetal position. Gabe walks around the bed and lays down behind me. He scoots close to me, spooning my body, his arm around my waist.

"I don't know what to say or do to make this any easier. Please, if there is anything, let me know," Gabe says quietly.

"Can I stay here with you for a few days? Just until I get my head straight," I say.

I hate the fact that I need him, but I do, and I hate having to ask for help but I can't do this alone.

"What do you mean stay here for a few days?" Gabe says. "You live here now, remember?"

"Yes, but that was when I was having a baby and we were going to be a family. You don't have to stay married to me now. I know this isn't what you signed up for," I say.

"Oh Clarissa," Gabe says. He holds me tighter for a second and then his grip relaxes again. "I know our wedding wasn't the most conventional wedding, but there wasn't a vow I said that I didn't mean. We're in this together and I will do anything to support you through this."

Hearing his words sends a fresh load of tears cascading down my face, but this time, they are different tears. I wouldn't say tears of happiness exactly – I am still far from happy – but they aren't tears of hurt either. I guess I could say that they are tears of relief maybe.

"Thank you," I say through the tears. I put my hand on his and leave it there. "I thought I lost both of you."

"You will never lose me," Gabe says. "Now close your eyes and try to rest."

I don't think I'll be able to fall asleep right now despite the exhaustion that has seeped into every part of my body, but I do as he says because I want to sleep. I want the oblivion it brings me. I close my eyes and force my tense shoulders to relax. Despite my skepticism, I fall asleep almost immediately, my body working with me for once.

23

GABE

I catch myself whistling as I fry bacon and I instantly stop myself. It doesn't seem right, me whistling away when I think about what Clarissa is going through. I think she had just gotten used to the idea of being pregnant and gotten to the point where she was looking forward to having a baby and then she lost it and it must have been a big shock to her system. I only wish I knew what to do to make her feel better. I don't know if there is anything that would help but if there is, I really hope she will let me know. I'm making her breakfast because it's the only thing I can think of to do, but that's nothing even close to doing enough to help her to get through this.

I still can't believe she thought she was going to lose me as well as her baby. As if I would leave because she's no longer pregnant. I mean I get it to an extent – that was the main reason she agreed to marry me in the first place – but I would never walk out on her, especially not when something like this has happened to her.

The bacon is almost cooked, and I go to the fridge and pull out a loaf of bread and a tub of butter. I take four slices of the bread out of the wrapper and spread butter thickly across them. I get two plates out and put two slices of the bread onto each plate. I go back to the bacon and turn the gas off and then I share the bacon between the two plates. I put it in the bread and cut the sandwiches into two.

I go to the fridge and put the bread and butter away and grab the ketchup. I put some of the ketchup on my sandwich and debate whether or not to add some to Clarissa's sandwich. She always liked ketchup before, but does she still eat it now? I have just decided that I'm going to put a squeeze on the side of her plate, and she can choose to eat it or not when a noise behind me startles me.

"Sorry. I didn't mean to make you jump," Clarissa says with a smile as I turn around.

"What are you doing up?" I ask.

"I'm going to get a shower and get ready for work," she says.

"Work? Are you kidding me?" I ask. I realize I'm still standing holding the ketchup bottle and I hold it up to Clarissa "Ketchup?"

"No thanks," she says. "And no, I'm not kidding you."

She sits down at the kitchen table, and I place her sandwich in front of her. I pour two mugs of coffee and put the ketchup back in the fridge. I put the mugs of coffee down on the table, one beside Clarissa and one beside my still empty seat, and then I sit down at the table opposite Clarissa with my own sandwich.

"You're not going to work today, Clarissa. You need to rest," I say.

"I look that bad huh?" she says.

She laughs and it's a fantastic sound and it makes me think that maybe she's healing. I decide to play along with her instead of trying to tell her that to me, she'll always be gorgeous.

"Well, I didn't want to say anything, but seeing as you've brought it up..." I trail off and we both laugh.

"Dick," Clarissa says.

"Is that an insult or a request?" I say with a raised eyebrow.

She laughs again, her hand over her mouth to hide her mouthful of sandwich. She chews and swallows.

"An insult," she says finally.

"Then consider me hurt," I say, pressing my hand on my heart.

We finish our sandwiches and Clarissa starts to get up.

"Do you want some more coffee?" she asks.

"Sit down. I'll get it," I say, jumping up.

She opens her mouth presumably to argue with me, but I already have both mugs and I'm halfway to the coffee maker, so she sits back down with a sigh.

"I can walk you know," she says. "It's not like I'm crippled. And no one is going to be running around after me at work like this."

I come back to the table with two fresh mugs of coffee and sit back down.

"You need to rest Clarissa. You don't have to come to work today," I say.

"But..." she starts.

"No buts. I'm sorry, I'm putting my foot down on this one," I say, interrupting her.

She raises an eyebrow at me.

"You really think I'm going to just sit here and let you tell me what to do? We might be married but you're not the boss of me," she says.

"On the contrary, in this situation, I am the boss. And

not because we're married, but because you work in my business. Look Clarissa I'm not just saying this to be an asshole you know," I say.

"I know you're not. I'm sorry. I shouldn't have said that. But seriously, I want to come to work. No one else would get special treatment," she says.

"No, they wouldn't get special treatment, but this isn't special treatment. This is a member of staff having a medical emergency and staying home sick the next few days. No one would think that was unreasonable," I say.

"But physically I feel ok," she says. "The cramps are no worse than my period cramps now."

"But your body went through trauma, Clarissa," I say.

I want to add that mentally I don't think she's ready to be around drunks, but I refrain from saying it, afraid that I will just annoy her if I say that.

"Ok, fine, I'll stay home," she says with a sigh.

"Thank you," I say.

I'm sure I see a look of relief on her face when she finally gives in, and it makes me glad that I pushed for her to stay home.

"Now get yourself back to bed," I tell her.

"I will," she says. "But I do need to shower first. I really think I'll feel better after a shower."

"Ok, shout at me if you need anything," I say.

"How loud do you think I can shout," she laughs. "You're due at the bar in like fifteen minutes."

"I'm not going in today. I'm staying home to look after you," I say.

"Oh no you're not," she says. I go to interrupt her, but she keeps going, not letting me get a word in. "And don't try to argue with me. I've given in and agreed to stay home. Now you have to meet me in the middle and accept that I don't need a babysitter. If I start to feel ill or anything, I promise I will call you. And you can't possibly say that you would do this for any other employee."

"I don't like the idea of leaving you alone," I say.

"Why? Are you scared I'll have a little look in your underwear drawer?" Clarissa asks, completely throwing me off my stride and making me laugh.

"Yes," I say. "I am terrified of that."

She laughs again.

"I promise I'll only have a quick look. How's that?" she says. We laugh again and then she turns serious. "Really though Gabe. I need things to go back to normal as soon as possible. I don't want to be all wrapped up in a case of self-pity, ok?"

"Ok," I say. I know the major thing was getting her to agree to stay home and I'm worried that if I push her, she will go back to insisting that she's going in for her shift. "But remember you promised to call me if you feel ill. I also need you to promise me you will call if you need anything at all."

"I promise," Clarissa says. "Now go before you're late."

"It's my bar. I can be late when I want to be," I say.

She shakes her head, her eyes twinkling with amusement.

"No. It's your bar so you have to set an example," she says.

24

GABE

I've been in the bar for about five minutes and already I'm distracted thinking about Clarissa. I feel like it was a mistake leaving her alone, but I knew she was right about meeting her halfway. I was afraid that if I didn't, she would turn up for her shift whether I liked it or not. I debate just leaving work again and going home but Clarissa is no idiot. She'll know I haven't had time to do anything I need to do and that I've just come home to be with her and then we'll probably have an argument.

No, instead of that, I'm going to work as quickly as I can so that I can get home to Clarissa but not give her any room to feel like I'm smothering her. With that in mind, I turn my attention to my computer and start working through my emails. I make good progress on those and then I move on to inputting the results of the inventory into the system and working out our profits for the month. It's been a good month money wise, and I'm pleased with the profits.

I hear Rebecca's voice coming from the staff break room and it reminds me that I need to speak to Penny about Friday. I buzz through to the bar and wait a second for

Penny to appear. I don't have to wait long before she taps on my door.

"Come in," I say.

Penny comes in and plonks herself down opposite me.

"What's up?" she asks.

"I've said Rebecca could have Friday off-" I start.

"Are you kidding me? She asked me for the day off and I said no because it's too short notice, so she's come running to you?" Penny says, cutting me off angrily.

"It's not like that Pen," I say. "She has a medical appointment that she said she didn't feel comfortable discussing with you."

"Oh ok," Penny says with a frown. "I can't imagine why she wasn't comfortable talking to me about it. Obviously if I had known she needed the day off for medical reasons I would have said yes. I'll try and figure something out, but I think we're going to be a bit short staffed."

"Just do the best you can," I say. "I can always jump on one of the bars if it comes to it."

Penny nods and leaves my office and I go back to my work. I'm seriously thinking of hiring someone else. I thought one extra member of staff would be enough when we took Clarissa on, but if Rebecca is going to be out at the hospital regularly then we're going to need her shifts covered. And also, if we start doing events, we'll need extra staff to cover those too.

I've been thinking for a while of putting on events. Nothing major at first. Maybe a weekly quiz night and then a band night or something like that. I have some research to do on costs and prices for those sorts of events, but I decide it can wait.

My security company is coming later on today to collect the weekly income and so I go to the safe and get all the money out. I count it up, label it, and put it in a secure bag. Now it's signed and sealed, Penny can deal with handing it over to the security firm.

I check the time. I'm surprised to see that almost four hours have passed since I first came in. I've done everything that needed to be done today and I think I've been here long enough for Clarissa to not think I'm rushing home to her. I start shutting down my computer when there's a tap on my office door.

"Come in," I shout.

The door opens and Rebecca comes in. She smiles at me, and I smile back.

"Are you ok?" I ask.

She nods her head and sits down without waiting to be asked to.

"Yes, I'm fine, thank you. I just wanted to say thank you again for being so understanding yesterday," she says. "About me needing Friday off. Penny just told me that it's sorted."

"Of course," I say. "No problem."

"And about the almost kiss," she says. I'm about to tell her not to worry about it thinking she is going to apologize again but instead; she shocks me to my core. "I get why you pushed me away. Like in case I thought you were trying to take advantage of me or something. But I don't see it that way. Honestly, you can kiss me right now and I won't think you're taking advantage of me. Or you can wait until I get the all clear and then we can be together if that makes you more comfortable."

I can't believe what I am hearing. The girl is seriously delusional. I don't want to have to be nasty to her, but it's starting to feel like that's the only way she will take the hint and leave me alone.

"Rebecca, that's not why I didn't kiss you. You know I'm married right?" I ask.

"Yes, I know all about your little pact and your fake wedding. Honestly, I don't mind that you did that while we were working towards getting together if you felt like it was something you had to do. But enough is enough. You can stop pretending the minister was real now," she says with a smile.

I feel like I'm banging my head against the wall.

"No Rebecca. It most definitely was not a fake wedding. The minister was very much real and so is our marriage," I say.

"Wow. You really did go the whole hog to keep a promise you made a long time ago didn't you," she says, shaking her head. "I mean I can't say that exactly fills me with joy but whatever, it's done now. I'm your future, not your past."

"No," I say firmly. "You are my employee and that's all it's ever going to be. I'm sorry Rebecca but I am married, and I intend to keep my wedding vows. And even aside from that, I don't have those kinds of feelings for you. I'm sorry but I just don't. This whole flirty, we're going to get together one day thing that you've got going on has to stop. Am I making myself clear?"

"Perfectly," Rebecca says coldly. I'm sure I see a flash of anger on her face but then she smiles, and I don't know whether I imagined the anger or whether the smile is fake. "I'm sorry. I get a little bit carried away sometimes. I really did think your marriage was just for show though, like the punchline to an old joke."

I really don't like the way she's talking about my wedding. I don't like the way her sweet smile doesn't quite reach her eyes either, but I let both of those things go. I can hardly tell her off for not being full of the joys of spring in the face of rejection and as for what she's saying about the wedding, I get the impression she's saying it for a reaction, and I am not about to play her games.

"Well now you know better, so I trust we won't have to have this conversation again," I say.

She nods her head and stands up.

"Yes. You've made yourself very clear," she replies. She starts for the door, but she stops when she reaches it. She turns her head to look at me and this time, her smile looks genuine. "If you change your mind, you know where to find me."

She's gone before I get over the shock of her last comment, so I don't reply. Once the door closes behind her, I just shake my head in disbelief. The girl is seriously starting to become too much. There is a line and I feel like she crosses it at least once per day. I decide that this is going to be her last warning. If she says or does anything else inappropriate, I am going to have to fire her. I know that will leave Penny in the shit a bit, but what else can I do?

The girl is harassing me, and I know for a fact if it was the other way around and I was the one harassing her, she would have likely gotten a restraining order against me by now. I'm not about to go and do that though even if I do end up having to fire her. I can handle her. It's not like she's violent or anything. She's more irritating than dangerous. I just don't want to ruin any chance I might have with Clarissa by having Rebecca hanging around me.

25

GABE

I ended up staying at the bar for another couple of hours after I wanted to because we are so short staffed. I've asked Penny to try and find at least one more bartender, maybe even two if she can. It's almost nine pm when I finally get back to the apartment.

I go in and peer into the living room. It's empty. I try the kitchen and that too is empty although I can see Clarissa has been busy. There's a prepared lasagna on the counter that looks like it just needs putting into the oven. I notice the sheet of paper beside the lasagna, and I feel a sense of dread. Has Clarissa gone out on her own? It's bad enough that she's been on her feet in the kitchen half the day making this but the thought of her being out on her own and maybe getting dizzy and not having anywhere to sit... I let the thought trail away. I don't want to think of Clarissa like that. I just hope she's back soon and ok. In the meantime, while I wait for her to come back home, I move over and pick up the piece of paper and read her note.

Gone for a nap. Can you put the lasagna in on two hundred and then wake me up please xo

I can't help but smile at the xo at the end of the note. I'm also smiling because I'm relieved to learn that Clarissa has only gone for a nap, she hasn't gone out for a walk or something and then been taken ill. This girl can keep me on my toes without even trying, it seems.

I turn the oven on and put the lasagna in it as she requested. I don't know how long she's been asleep for and to be honest, I'm tempted to leave her – she needs to rest – but she did ask me to wake her up and she also needs to eat. I decide to do as she has asked, and I head out into the hallway and towards the bedrooms at the end. I see that the door to Clarissa's bedroom is open, and she isn't in there. I smile to myself. She must have gotten back into my bed. I love that she feels like that's the place she can get comfort.

I tap lightly on my bedroom door just in case she's up and changing or anything. There's no answer so I push the door open. Clarissa is laid on her side facing the door. She is sound asleep, her mouth open and a little bit of drool running down her chin. Her eyes are rolling beneath the lids as she dreams. Even like that she is stunning to me.

I move over to the bed and touch her shoulder. She moans but she doesn't open her eyes. I shake her gently.

"Clarissa," I say. "I'm back."

"Hmm," she says.

Her eyes flicker open and she smiles up at me but then they close again and stay that way. I sit down on the side of the bed beside her and decide I'm going to try one more time and if she still doesn't wake up, I'm going to assume that her body needs sleep more than it needs food at the minute.

"Clarissa? Dinner's in the oven," I say.

Her eyes open again and this time, she seems to focus on

me properly. She groans and runs her hands over her eyes and then she wipes the drool from her chin. She sits up facing me, her body only inches from mine.

"How long have I been asleep?" she asks.

"I have no idea," I say. "I've just gotten in and saw your note. It's just after nine."

"Nine at night?" she says, clearly still a bit befuddled and not quite awake properly yet. I nod and she shakes her head. "Wow. I think it was about three when I came to take a nap."

"Do you feel better after getting some sleep?" I ask.

She's silent for a moment, seemingly considering my question. She nods her head.

"Yes. Actually, I do," she says with a smile.

"Good," I say.

Without thinking, I reach out and caress her cheek with the palm of my hand. She snuggles against it, and I leave it there. She looks up at me and for a second, everything stops still as we look into each other's eyes. Before I can stop myself, I'm leaning in and kissing Clarissa. She kisses me back and her arms wrap around me. I bring my other hand up and push it into her hair. My tongue slips into her mouth and her tongue collides with it. She moans into my mouth as we kiss, our hunger for each other clear in the passion within our kiss.

I'm shocked when Clarissa pulls away from the kiss abruptly, but then I kick myself mentally. I shouldn't have done that. She's still grieving, and I have taken advantage of her. I'm a horrible person and I hate myself for what I've done.

"I am so sorry," I say.

"It's fine," Clarissa says. She scoots backwards a bit and then she moves her legs around and gets out of the bed leaving me sitting there alone. "It was as much my fault as yours."

I don't really believe that but it's sweet of her to say it.

"I feel awful. You need a friend right now, not this," I say.

She smiles at me and offers me her hand. I take it and she pulls me up off the bed and gives me a quick hug.

"Honestly, it's fine. Please don't feel bad about it," she says. "Now come on, let's go and get our dinner. I'm starving."

I follow her out of the bedroom and along the hallway to the kitchen, forcing myself not to watch the way her hips sway slightly with each step she takes.

"I'm pretty hungry too. And I've seen the size of that lasagna, so you can be sure I won't have the energy to be kissing you tonight," I say, trying to reassure her that I won't be trying anything with her again but also trying to make a joke of the situation so that it doesn't get any more awkward.

"I think I should be going back to my own bed tonight," she says.

I feel broken at her words. She needs my support and now she doesn't want to even be around me in case I touch her inappropriately.

"Honestly Clarissa, you don't have to do that. I promise you I won't touch you," I say.

We're in the kitchen now and she smiles at me over her shoulder before she bends down and opens the oven door to check the lasagna.

"I wish I could make the same promise, but I can't and I'm not in the right place to test my will power right now," she says.

I honestly don't know what to say to that, so I don't say anything. Even if she has just said it to let me off the hook, it's worked. I don't feel half as bad about instigating our kiss now I know that Clarissa doesn't think she can stop herself from kissing me or more if we end up in the same bed together tonight.

26

CLARISSA

I lay awake staring up at the ceiling. I've been in every position imaginable since coming to bed but no matter what I do, I can't get comfortable enough to sleep. I keep trying to tell myself it's because of my extra-long nap I had earlier, but I know that's not the reason for my insomnia. Not really although honestly it probably didn't help.

The main reason for my insomnia tonight is simple. I miss Gabe being beside me. I miss the warmth of his body, the love in his touch. I want to be back in his room, back in his arms. I want him to kiss me all over and make love to me. I want us to lock ourselves away in a little bubble and pretend we are on our honeymoon again so that we can do whatever we want to do with each other's bodies.

But I can't let myself go to him. Not now. It's for the same reason as I pulled away from his kiss earlier. When Gabe kissed me, it felt right. It felt like our lips were made to fit together and I never wanted to let him go. But as I melted into him, I felt a sharp tug of guilt in my stomach and that was what made me pull away and it's what is stopping me from going to him now.

It feels wrong, me letting myself be happy, letting myself enjoy human touch when I have just lost my baby. I feel like I'm somehow sullying his or her memory, like I'm not grieving properly. I should be lying in bed crying not lying in bed being fucked.

I know I should give myself a break. I know I have to move on. But not yet. I need to take some time just for myself where I think about what could have been with Gabe, the baby and me becoming a little family. And once I've played that fantasy out in my head, watched the baby grow up there, maybe then I will be able to let go of the pain of the loss and then who knows what might happen between Gabe and me.

I hope he doesn't feel too bad about kissing me. I know when I pulled away how guilty he felt. It was written all over his face. I did try to reassure him that he had nothing to feel guilty about, but then when I said I could no longer share his bed, I saw that look on his face again, the look of a man who is tormenting himself. That's why I said what I said about me not being sure I can control myself. I mean I'm not sure I can. I think being close to Gabe affects me in more ways than one. But I also said it so that he knows that this isn't me punishing him for getting too close.

I don't really know how everything became such a mess. I just wish I could go back in time and do it all differently.

27

CLARISSA

By the time Gabe gets up today, I've been in the shower and washed and dried my hair, put makeup on, and dressed in a black wrap dress. I have also texted Penny to let her know I will be in today. She seemed pretty relieved, texting me back to say she's got Rebecca and a new starter in and there's a christening party on from twelve until three.

I've also made breakfast for us both – pancakes and maple syrup – and Gabe smiles when he comes into the kitchen and sees the pile of pancakes in the center of the table. His smile fades when he looks at me.

"What's with the dress?" he says.

"I'm coming back to work," I reply as I reach for a pancake. "And please don't try to talk me out of it. It's been nearly a week now and it's time, Gabe. I'll go mad if I sit around here any longer."

"Ok," Gabe agrees. "I can see you've made your mind up but can we agree that you'll be on light duties for the first few days at least?"

"Well, there's three of us on the bar today, me, Rebecca

and a new starter, and it's a christening so hopefully it won't be too rowdy," I reply.

"How do you know all of that?" Gabe asks.

I look down at the table, feeling my cheeks turning pink with the rush of blood that flies to them. I've stepped right in it now and I'm a bit ashamed to tell him what I've done. I'm going to have to now though.

"I was worried you would try and stop me from coming back to work so I sent a text message to Penny and said I'd be in today," I admit.

"Because you knew I wouldn't want to then have to go to Penny and say I talked you out of coming in," Gabe says.

I nod sheepishly, but he doesn't look angry. Instead, he laughs.

"Well, I have to admit I admire your spunk," he laughs. "What time did you tell her you'd be there?"

"The christening starts at twelve so around eleven thirty she said," I tell him.

Gabe checks his watch.

"Oh, we have plenty of time to kill then," he says. He looks at me and laughs. "You can tell me about any other times you've gone over my head."

THE SECOND GABE and I walk into the bar Penny comes rushing over to us. She pulls me into a hug which I return.

"It's so good to see you," she says. "How are you feeling?"

"She needs to be on light duties," Gabe says before I can speak.

I roll my eyes.

"I'm fine thank you," I tell Penny. "I'm still getting my head around what happened, but physically I'm fine and I couldn't face another day just sitting there moping around the apartment."

"Well, it sure is good to have you back," Penny says. "All I want you to do today is serve behind the bar. No carrying trays of cans and bottles or baskets of glasses. Do you hear me?"

I nod.

"Good," she says. "Rebecca has been told you're not to do any of the running and if you feel like you need to sit down, just say."

I nod again.

"Thank you but I'm sure I won't," I say.

"Wait," Gabe says. "How come when Penny says something you're agreeable, but when I say something, you fight me every step of the way?"

"Because Penny isn't going to try and wrap me up in bubble wrap and have me never leave the apartment again," I say.

Gabe shakes his head but he's laughing. I spot Rebecca heading towards us and I cringe inside, but she smiles at me and reaches out and rubs the top of my arm quickly.

"Are you ok? I'm so sorry about what happened to you," she says.

"Thanks," I say. "I'm getting there."

"Well, if there's anything I can do, just let me know, ok?" she says.

I nod, surprised at this apparent change in her. She must feel really sorry for me to go from how cold she was before the miscarriage to this now.

"Where's Jamie?" Penny asks Rebecca.

"I asked him to go and grab a tray of tonics from the cellar," Rebecca says.

"Ok. When he comes back, I'll introduce him to Clarissa," Penny says.

"Are we not working upstairs in the function room with it being a christening?" I ask.

"No. It's so quiet on a Monday afternoon we're just having it down here," she says. "The dad of the baby is a regular and he's fine with it if a couple of people come in who aren't with the party."

A voice shouts Penny's name.

"Oh, that's the DJ," she says. "Please excuse me. I'm sure Rebecca can introduce you to Jamie."

She flits off leaving Gabe and me alone except for Rebecca who is behind the bar at the opposite end of the room. We make our way down that way.

"What needs to be done before we open?" I ask Rebecca.

"Nothing," she says. "We're all set up. There're just a few bottles of tonic to put in the fridge but I can do that. I wanted to get it all done so you didn't feel like you had to do any of it."

"Thank you but I'm here to work," I say.

"On light duties," Gabe adds.

I roll my eyes but before I can chastise him, a young man appears with a tray of tonic in his hand. He smiles at me and Gabe and Rebecca waves her hand in our direction.

"That's Clarissa, another bartender. And Gabe, the owner," she says.

"Hi," Jamie says smiling over at us as Rebecca takes the tonic from him. "I'm Jamie."

"Welcome to the team Jamie," Gabe says. "I'll speak to you properly later on; I just have a call I have to make." He turns to me. "Remember what I said about light duties."

I nod and tell him to go. He looks at me for a moment

like he's about to say something else but then he goes off towards the door leading to the hallway with his office in it.

"So, Jamie, you know how pregnant women can't lift things?" Rebecca says without looking up from the fridge she's restocking with the tonic bottles.

"Yeah," Jamie says and nods his head.

"Well around here, apparently they still can't lift anything or do much of anything useful even once they're not pregnant anymore," she adds.

My jaw drops. I can't believe she's just said that. My hands ball into fists at my sides and I clench them so hard that I can feel my nails almost puncturing my palms. It's either that or I'll be hopping over the bar and punching Rebecca. The truth is that's exactly what I would like to do but I don't want to give her the satisfaction of thinking that she's got to me.

Jamie is looking down at the ground, obviously uncomfortable with Rebecca's little announcement. Rebecca closes the fridge door.

"I'm going to get some more stuff," she says.

She disappears through the door, and I hear her feet clattering on the cellar steps. I smile at Jamie, trying to smooth over the awkwardness.

"Have you worked in a bar before?" I ask.

He nods his head.

"Yeah. Well, it was a night club actually, but same sort of thing," he says with another smile.

"Oh, you'll be fine here then. We do get busy on the weekends and some evenings but obviously it's nothing compared to a nightclub," I tell him. "Still though if you do have any questions or anything, just let me or Rebecca know."

"Rebecca doesn't give me the impression she's the most helpful person," Jamie says.

It takes all the willpower I have not to hug him. I laugh softly instead.

"It's just me she has a problem with. She's absolutely fine with everyone else so I'm sure she would help you," I say.

"So, you're the one who just had the baby? Who Rebecca was talking about earlier? How long have you been back to work?" he asks.

"It's my first day back. But I didn't have a baby. I had a miscarriage," I say.

It's the first time I've said that out loud and it sends a rush of pain through my whole body. I swallow it down. Poor Jamie is already uncomfortable enough without me bursting into tears through our conversation.

"What? You lost your baby and she's making snotty remarks about you?" Jamie says, looking horrified. "Can you not report her or anything?"

"I mean I could but she's not important enough to me for me to be bothered by her comments," I say and as I say it, I realize it's the truth. Rebecca can't hurt me. She doesn't matter to me in any way, and I have to have some respect for someone for their words to hurt me.

"Fair enough," Jamie says. "But I don't think that's very nice of her at all."

I need to move this conversation on. I don't want it to look like I'm trying to poison the new person against Rebecca. I'm relieved when I spot the time – it's a minute to twelve.

"I'll go and get the doors open," I say. "The christening party is expected around twelve."

I go and unlock the main door to the bar and push it

open. I turn back and walk towards the bar. I go behind it and grab a cloth and begin to wash down the bar top. Rebecca has come back up from the cellar while I've been opening the door and she's just finished refilling the last few rows of bottles in the fridge. She turns to me and smirks.

"Are you sure that's not too hard for you?" she sneers.

"Oh, I'm sure if you can do it I can too," I reply, faking a smile.

Customers are starting to come into the bar now and Rebecca doesn't get a chance to fire anything clever back at me. The three of us are soon in the routine of serving the customers. After the first wave of a rush, it calms down a little bit. From nowhere, Rebecca comes over to me and wraps her arm around my shoulders.

"If you're in pain, you should sit down," she says.

I have no idea where this is coming from, but it doesn't sound sarcastic like she did earlier. Maybe it's her way of apologizing for that.

"I'm not in pain," I say. "Honest, I'm fine."

"You don't have to lie just because Gabe is here," she says. "He won't think any less of you for being human."

Oh, so that's her game. She's going to be a complete dick to me but kiss my ass whenever Gabe appears. Well, she can get fucked if she thinks I'm going to play along with that. I shrug her arm off my shoulders.

"I said I'm fine," I repeat.

"Ok sorry," Rebecca says, backing away from me with a hurt look on her face.

Little bitch. I turn towards Gabe who is frowning in my direction.

"Clarissa, have you got a minute?" he says.

"Not really," I reply. "Jamie has gone for his break, and I don't want to leave Rebecca on the bar alone."

"Oh, I'm ok, go ahead," Rebecca says. She's standing where I can see her, but Gabe can't and the smug smile on her face makes me want to go over there and slap her stupid face.

I roll my eyes and follow Gabe into the hallway behind the bar.

"I'm fine," I say before Gabe can say anything. "I'm not in pain."

"Well ok, but you could have handled that better. Rebecca was just being nice," he says.

I laugh and shake my head.

"I know girls like Rebecca. Trust me when I say she wasn't being nice," I tell him.

I can see by the way he looks at me that he doesn't really believe me, but I refuse to have an argument with him about it here. I won't give that bitch the satisfaction of thinking she's come between Gabe and me. We will be having a serious talk about it tonight though.

I go back behind the bar and Gabe comes through and heads for the stairs. When he's gone, I smile after him so Rebecca can see.

"Aww he just wanted to make sure I was ok. He's so sweet," I say.

I can almost feel the anger coming off Rebecca in waves, but if she wants to play stupid games with me, then I'll play them with her. I'm done being nice to her or trying to get her to at least be civil to me.

The christening party goes really well. The guests are big drinkers so there is always someone at the bar, but they seem like the kind of people who can handle their drinks and there's no trouble or even the sense that trouble is looming. I make a fortune in tips and I'm sure Rebecca and Jamie do too. Jamie seems to be doing well. He's definitely hit the ground running. Over the course of the shift, when-ever Gabe has been in sight, Rebecca has been as sweet as pie to me asking me if I'm ok, if I need to sit down or a glass of water or a bit of fresh air. Whenever he hasn't been in sight, she's had something snarky to say, but to be honest, her words are having little effect on me. I don't want to be friends with someone like her and I don't care enough about her to care what she may or may not think of me.

At a couple of minutes to three, the father of the child who has been christened comes up to the bar. There is no sign of the baby or any other children which at first, I found strange, but I have since discovered that the actual chris-tening was yesterday, which makes a lot more sense having it on a Sunday rather than on a Monday. They had a big party then and the children were there. This is a second celebration for the people who couldn't be there, and the grandmother of the baby has the children today.

"Thank you, ladies and gentlemen, for your service this afternoon," the father of the baby says. "If it was up to me, we'd be staying here but we have tables booked at a restau-rant and the wife is giving me that 'don't you dare' look."

He laughs and we do too.

"Seriously though, you've all been fantastic. Thanks again," he says. He puts his hand into his pants pocket and pulls out three fifty dollar bills and puts them on the bar. "One each."

We all thank him, and the group gets up and leaves the bar leaving it completely empty except for a pair of regulars who have been sitting right at the back of the room out of the way of the celebration but are now moving into the main part of the room.

I look out into the area the big group has vacated. A mess is the wrong word – it's not like there's broken glass all over or anything – but they have left a ton of empty glasses and bottles.

"I'll go and start collecting all of that in," I say.

"Are you sure you should be doing that?" Jamie says.

"Sure," I say. "As I was reminded earlier on, it's only while you're pregnant you can't lift anything."

Jamie looks seriously uncomfortable, and I instantly regret bringing him into whatever the hell is going on between Rebecca and me. I smile at him.

"Thank you though. Do you want to start washing what I bring back?" I ask.

Jamie smiles back and nods his head and I leave the bar and start collecting the empties. I take the first load back to the bar. I start unloading them in the glass washing area.

"Where is Rebecca anyway?" Jamie asks me.

"I'm not sure to be honest," I say. "She might have gone on her break."

It would have been common courtesy if she'd told us where she was going. I know she's no fan of me, but she doesn't have to be a fan of me to work efficiently with me. And she has no reason to dislike Jamie surely so she could have told him where she was going.

"Actually, I was down in the cellar getting some stock," Rebecca says, appearing back behind the bar with a couple of trays of bottles.

"Oh ok, thank you," I say. I actually mean that. I hate carting the trays up and down the stairs. "Did you want to go on your break now that it's quiet or did you want to wait?"

"Well seeing as how you're not my boss, I don't think I have to answer that one to you," Rebecca says.

"Ok, fuck you then," I say, sick to death of playing nice with her.

I turn from the bar and go back to collecting up the

empties. I take another arm load back to the glass washing area. Rebecca comes towards the area. I wish I could just walk away but I can't because I still have a ton of glasses in my arms.

"I'll be out to help you in a second when I've restocked the fridges," she says. She reaches beneath the bar and comes up with a big silver tray. "If you take this it's much easier and you don't have to press the glasses against your clothes where people's mouths have been."

She gives me a small smile and pushes the tray towards me. I unload the last glasses and pick it up.

"Thanks," I say.

I look around for Gabe but he's nowhere to be seen and I feel shocked. Why is Rebecca being nice to me all of a sudden? Has she realized that she's gone too far, or has she just realized that I'm not going to be intimidated by her? Whatever. I decide I will treat her as she treats me. While she's being civil or even nice to me, I'll be civil back. When she's being an asshole to me, I'll be an asshole back to her. I'm not going to waste my time trying to work her out anymore.

I go back to the used tables and load up the tray. I have to admit that Rebecca was right. This is much easier, and it does save the dirty glasses from touching me. I've lost count of the number of times I've ended up with lipstick marks on my clothes where the rims of glasses have rubbed against me as I was carrying a stack of them.

I go back to the bar and empty the tray. I spot Gabe coming out of the bar as I head back out again. Rebecca comes out with me this time. The cynic in me wants to think it's because she's spotted Gabe, but I have to give her the benefit of the doubt because she did say she'd be coming to help me once the fridges were restocked, and she has just finished doing them.

We both start to load up our trays. I have mine almost full when Gabe comes over.

"You shouldn't be out here collecting these," Gabe said. "You were meant to be staying behind the bar."

"I told her, but she wouldn't listen," Rebecca says.

Fucking little liar.

"Guys seriously I'm fine. I don't need special treatment. I'm quite capable of collecting a few glasses. It's not like it's busy or anything and I'm going to be getting shoved around," I say.

I've still been filling up my tray as I talk and rather than trying to argue with me, Gabe just picks the tray up himself and takes it to the bar for me. I roll my eyes at his antics. I start to turn around to head back to the bar myself when Rebecca barges into me hard enough that I stumble. Time seems to slow down. The tray of glasses in her hands slips and tumbles to the ground with the loudest smashing sound. It sounds like all the windows are breaking at once.

The glasses and the tray hit the ground and I realize I'm still falling. I tried to grab a chair back as I stumbled but I missed my grip and I'm falling to the ground, to the glass. I land hard on my hands and knees. My hands are clear of the glass, but I feel a searing pain in one of my knees.

The second I hit the ground, time speeds back up to normal speed. Gabe, Jamie and the regular couple have all heard the smashing sound and watched me fall and all four of them are running towards me. Rebecca has her hand in my armpit and the other holds my hand as she tries to get me off the ground.

The couple reach us first and they help Rebecca get me up. Gabe and Jamie reach us all as I'm lifted to my feet.

"Thank you," I say to the couple. "Talk about clumsy huh."

"Well, it was hardly your fault dear," the woman says. "Rebecca knocked you flying."

"Did you?" Gabe demands, fixing Rebecca with a look so full of anger I think he might fire her on the spot.

"Yes, but I didn't mean to. It was an accident. I tripped and I thought I was going to drop the tray, so I sort of flicked my arm to keep it from going and my arm hit Clarissa," she says. She turns to look at me. "I am so, so sorry."

"It's ok. I'm ok," I say.

"I don't think you are," Jamie puts in. He nods towards my knees, and I look down and see a lump of glass sticking out of my knee, blood running down my leg.

"It's nothing," I say.

I reach down and pull out the lump of glass and that's when I realize how deep the cut is. I can see the white of bone beneath the open flesh.

"That needs stitches," Gabe says. "Come on. I'll drive you to the emergency room. Jamie, can you run upstairs and tell Penny what's happened please."

Jamie nods and goes towards the stairs.

"Rebecca, can you clean this up please," Gabe says.

She nods her head and when she speaks, her voice is practically a whisper.

"I really am sorry Clarissa," she says.

"It's ok," I tell her.

"Let's go," Gabe says, patting his pockets and pulling his car keys out.

He's a few steps ahead and there is just Rebecca and me there and she gives me this smile. It's a cold smile, a smile that says I can do what I want to you and get away with it. And that's when I know her apology was fake. That was no accident. She meant for me to fall. For the first time, I feel icy fingers of fear caressing the back of my neck. How far will Rebecca go to get rid of me and try to get Gabe?

I don't even want to think about it, so I hurry to catch up with Gabe. It hurts to walk, and I feel a fresh spurt of blood with each step, but I know if I say anything, Gabe is likely to pick me up and carry me out to his car and that would just be too embarrassing.

We leave the bar and head towards the parking lot. I'm aware that this is how my last shift ended too with us heading to the parking lot so that Gabe could take me to the emergency room. At least this time there's no baby to lose. Getting a few stitches is nothing.

"Rebecca looked mortified about your leg," Gabe says as we get into the car.

"So, she should," I snort. "She did that on purpose."

I'm done covering for her, especially now that I really think she might be dangerous.

"Don't be silly," Gabe says.

"I'm not being fucking silly," I snap. I sigh. "Sorry. It's not your fault. I know that. But she did do it on purpose. You didn't see the way she smiled at me when you turned your back. It was a cold fucking evil smile."

"Are you sure it wasn't just because she felt guilty?" he says.

"I'm sure. Come on Gabe, you know she hates me," I say.

"She doesn't hate you," Gabe replies. "Look I know she had a crush on me at one point but that's over and done with now. She doesn't act like someone who hates you. I think she's really making an effort and it would actually be good if you could do the same."

I know then I'm not going to convince him of Rebecca's utter dislike for me. If I start telling him everything she has said and done it's either going to sound like I'm making it up or he's going to be upset that I kept all of this from him. I sigh and sit back in the seat.

"I do make an effort with her," I say. "And believe me I'll be making more of an effort after this or who knows what she'll do next."

"I think maybe your hormones are still a bit all over the place Clarissa. Honestly, you should hear yourself. You're talking like she's some sort of lunatic. She's harmless," he says.

I bite my tongue to not snap at him again. I know when something is my hormones making me feel bad and when someone is actively taunting me. But I'm not going to go there. I'm not about to get into an argument with Gabe and give Rebecca exactly what she wants.

28

GABE

"Are you sure you don't mind waiting?" I ask Clarissa. "It's going to be well over an hour and if you don't want to hang about here, I can ask Penny to drop you off at home. She won't mind. She's already said she doesn't mind."

"No, it's fine, I don't mind waiting," Clarissa says.

"Ok, if you're sure, let me just go and tell Penny she can go," I say.

Clarissa nods her head and I leave my office and go off to find Penny and tell her she can go home. One of us has to be here but there's no reason at all for her to be here too. The bar is closed but the alarm won't set and if I leave it unset and anything happens, my insurance is void so I've had to call the alarm company and have them send an engineer out to fix the panel. They've said it will be at least an hour's wait which is why I asked Clarissa if she wanted to go home now rather than hang around waiting for me. It's a long time to just hang around when it's already late.

If it had been closer to the miscarriage, I would have insisted on her leaving, but it's been two months and she seems to be back to her old self again. I know she still has her moments where the loss hits her and I'm sure that will be true for a long time to come, but physically, she's fine now and I don't feel like she's fragile mentally anymore. I think she has coped so well with all of this, and I'm so proud of her for picking herself back up after the tragedy.

"Hey," I say when I find Penny standing in the doorway smoking a cigarette. "You get yourself home. Clarissa wants to wait but thanks for offering to take her home."

"No worries. See you tomorrow then," she says.

She steps outside and I wave her off and lock the front door behind her. I turn around to find Clarissa sitting at one of the tables. She smiles at me, and I head over to her.

"I prefer to sit out here rather than in your office if it's all the same to you," she says.

"Sure," I agree and sit down next to her. "Whatever you want."

"I actually wanted to talk to you about something," she says.

"Ok," I say. "Go on." She doesn't speak immediately, and I reach out and rub her arm. "It's ok. You can talk to me about anything."

She flashes me a smile and nods her head.

"I know I can. Because you're my best friend. But you're more than that. Or at least I want you to be... I... I think I'm ready. For a relationship I mean," she says.

For a moment, I don't speak. I don't know what to say because I don't quite know if she's telling me that she's ready for a relationship with me or if she's telling me that she's ready for a relationship, so we need to get divorced.

Assuming you still want to, of course," she says flashing me another sheepish little smile. "And I mean if you don't want to, I understand, you just have to say because-

I could let her go on. She's cute and flustered and I'm quite enjoying it but I can't wait another minute and I kiss her, cutting off her words. Our kiss is loving and tender, full of everything we want to say. When we pull apart, I smile at Clarissa.

"I still want to," I say.

"Oh good," Clarissa says. "You had me kind of worried there."

"No need to worry on my account," I laugh. "I've been in since... well since... forever I guess."

"Can we take it slow though?" Clarissa says.

"Of course," I say. "So should we get divorced then?"

Clarissa laughs and playfully punches me in the arm.

"You know what I mean," she laughs.

I don't really know if I do know what she means or not but as long as I get to be with her, we can go at whatever pace she wants to. I will just follow her lead. She gets up and moves towards the jukebox.

"We need music," she announces.

She puts a coin in and chooses a song. Lady Gaga's "Bad Romance" blasts from the speakers and I wince slightly.

"Maybe not the best choice," I say.

"It's not about us," Clarissa says with a laugh. "I just like the song. It makes me want to dance."

She's halfway between the jukebox and the table I'm sitting at. She stops walking and starts swaying her hips. She puts her arms up and sways and spins, throwing her head back and letting the music take her. God she is sexy. The only reason I stop myself from going to her is because I'm enjoying the show too much.

She's working herself into a frenzy and then she grabs the bottom of her dress and pulls it over her head. She keeps dancing, standing there in just her underwear and I feel my cock hardening at the sight of her and although I still want to watch her dance, I can't wait any longer to go to her and touch her.

I get up off my chair and go to her. She watches me approaching her, her eyes filled with lust and her chest heaving. I reach her and wrap my arms around her waist and lift her. She barely weighs anything, and she comes up easily. She wraps her arms around my shoulders and her legs around my waist and our lips find each other once more.

Clarissa clings to me as our kiss explodes with passion. Our tongues collide and caress each other and I run my hands over the bare skin of her back and then further down until I'm cupping her ass cheeks in my hands. I walk towards the bar with her in my arms. When I reach it, I set her down on the edge of it and pull back from her slightly. I push her legs open and push her panties to one side and then I step in between her legs and begin to lick her clit.

She moans, sitting back, taking her weight on her hands and opening herself up to me. She hooks one leg around my shoulders as I work her. I bring her to the edge of her climax and then I stop and pull back, gently disentangling myself from her leg. I grab her ass and pull her towards me again and she comes willingly, jumping into my arms once more.

I pull her panties off her ass and then I turn with her and sit her on the nearest table. I peel her panties the rest of the way down her legs and off her feet and then I pull her into my arms again and kiss her hard on the mouth. I release her long enough to open my jeans and push them down along with my boxer shorts and then I'm inside Clarissa and we are moving as one, pleasure flowing through my cock and into my stomach and the rest of my body.

I kiss along Clarissa's cheek, down her neck and across her collar bone as I fill her up and move inside of her. She grips me tighter, her nails digging into my shoulders. I'm so close to climaxing that when Clarissa says my name in a breathy voice, I can't stop myself from coming. Clarissa's pussy tightens around my cock as I spasm inside of her. We hold each other tightly, our shared orgasm uniting us in body, mind and soul.

As my orgasm fades, I slip out of Clarissa, and we hold each other. Finally, I stand back and pull my jeans and boxer shorts back up. Clarissa hops off the table and gets back into her panties. She has just settled them into place when a loud knock comes from the front door.

"Alarm engineer," a voice shouts.

"Fuck, my dress," Clarissa says, darting across the bar.

I watch her ass jiggle in her panties. I don't head for the door until she has her dress back on and even then, I'm tempted to send the engineer away so that Clarissa and I can make love once more.

29

CLARISSA

Gabe and I are sitting side by side in his apartment watching a movie. It's late – we've not long finished work – and the movie is boring me. I think about going to bed but then I have a better idea. Instead of standing up, I slip off the couch and kneel on the ground.

"Are you ok?" Gabe says, looking down at me on the ground.

I don't reply. I just smile up at him as I move closer to him. I reach for the button on his jeans and open it and then I pull his zipper down. When I hook my fingers into his waistband, he lifts his ass and I peel his jeans and boxer shorts down his legs in one swift movement. I pause for long enough to pull his shoes and socks off and then I finish stripping him of his jeans and boxer shorts.

I push his knees open and crawl between them and then I lean forward and take his cock into my mouth. As soon as the tip touches my lips, Gabe's cock hardens. I put my lips over my teeth and suck the tip into my mouth. Gabe's groan of pleasure makes my pussy ache, but this is about him not me. He always gives me the most amazing oral sex and I think it's about time I returned the favor.

I suck him into my mouth and bob my head up and down, running my lips over his length. I come up and release him from my mouth, holding the base of his cock in one fist. I lick the tip, flicking my tongue back and forth over it and planting tiny kisses on it. Gabe moans again and I run my tongue down his length and then lick him like an ice cream.

I love the musky, salty taste of him in my mouth and I suck him back in. I hold his cock in my mouth and run my hands beneath his t-shirt and over his belly and sides, a light, teasing touch. I move them back down, still sucking on him. I rest my hands on his hips and then I release his cock again and move my attention to his inner thighs. I lick up one and down the other one and then I come back in a series of kisses. I nip his skin gently between my teeth.

When I get back to his cock, I see that his hands are balled into fists at his sides, and I smile to myself. I love knowing that I can have that effect on him. I plunge my mouth over him, taking his full length in and then I begin to suck on him hard while moving my head up and down. Gabe thrusts his hips beneath me, and I can hardly breathe but I don't care, I just want to make him feel as good as he makes me feel.

I keep sucking, keep moving and finally, I'm rewarded with Gabe calling out my name, his back arching, and his cum flooding my mouth. I swallow it and keep sucking and swallowing, drinking him dry as he writhes beneath my mouth.

When he's done, I get back up off the floor still without saying a word and sit back down beside Gabe. He grins at me and shakes his head.

"We should watch movies you're not into more often," he says with a soft laugh.

I laugh and nod.

"Well hopefully that was better than the movie," I say.

"Of course," Gabe says. "We can turn it off if you want to - you know."

"No, it's fine," I say, shaking my head.

Gabe stands up and puts his clothes back on and then I lay down on the couch with my head on his lap. I try to get into the movie but it's just not happening, and my mind starts to wander.

I smile to myself remembering how I asked Gabe if we could take things slowly. I don't even know what I meant by that myself. In other circumstances it would have made sense, but it made no sense at all in our situation. How can you take it slowly with someone when you're already living with them and are already married to them?

It's been a month since we had that conversation and it's been anything but slow between us. We have hardly spent a moment apart except for when one of us is at work and the other has the day off. I must admit I was a little bit worried that living together and working together would be too much once we started to become a couple but it's not at all. It's nice having Gabe around all the time and to be honest, I don't see that much of him at work anyways. We take our breaks together but that's about it.

I hope Gabe is in the same place as I am where he accepts that we haven't gone slowly at all, but he's cool with it and happy with the way things are going. I would like that at any time, but I think more so than ever I need that to be the case now, because I've missed another period.

I know he was happy enough to be a father to my other baby, so I think he'll be happy to be a father to his own baby.

I want to tell him now, but I don't want to get his hopes up and then find out that I'm wrong. I'm going to do a test in the morning while he's at work and then hopefully, I will get to give him the good news when he gets back home after his shift.

30

GABE

I check my watch. Another hour or so and then I think I'll split. It's after nine and it's not massively busy and I can't see it getting much busier now. I'm sure the staff that are in can handle it and Penny is here to lock up.

I'm looking forward to getting home to Clarissa. To be honest, I would have sort of expected a bit of the newness to have worn off by now and going home to her would just be part of my routine but that's not the case at all. I still count down the hours until I can see her again and I still get butterflies in my stomach whenever she walks into a room.

I suppose some people would say it's kind of pathetic, but I don't care what those people say. I have never been in love like this before and I never want to be without Clarissa ever again. I want to tell her all of this, but I agreed when she asked if we could take it slowly. We already live together, we're already married. This is the one place we can take things slow by not throwing the L word around too soon. I can live with keeping my feelings to myself and I will tell Clarissa how I feel down the line when the time is right.

I stop daydreaming about Clarissa when I hear shouting

coming from the bar. It's not unusual for people to get louder when they're drinking but this sounds like angry shouting. I get up and go and open my office door.

"Are you some sort of fucking idiot? Is the simplest thing too goddamn hard for you?" I hear a male voice shouting.

It's definitely angry shouting. I leave my office and hurry down the hallway to the bar. As I step into the bar area, I take in the scene. Rebecca is on the bar and Tania is out collecting glasses down at the bottom of the bar. She, like most of the customers, are staring in shock at the man standing at the bar yelling at Rebecca.

"What's wrong? Are you too stupid to even answer me?" the man yells. He slams his fist down on the bar when Rebecca still doesn't respond. She's just looking at him, the fear on her face clear to see. "Answer me you ignorant little bitch."

"That's enough," I say. My voice is louder than my usual speaking voice, but I'm not quite shouting. "What on earth is going on here?"

"Apparently you employ idiots, that's what's going on," the man says.

I ignore him completely and focus on Rebecca.

"What happened?" I ask my voice more gentle now.

"He asked for a vodka and Coke, and I accidentally put lemonade in it instead," she says.

"Did you change the drink when this was pointed out to you?" I ask.

Rebecca nods.

"Ok," I say. "Go have a break, I'll take care of this."

I turn to face the customer who is smirking like he just won some sort of prize.

"Get out," I say.

I'm aware that Rebecca is still standing behind the bar at

first. When I tell the customer to get out, she seems to relax a little bit and then she disappears out the back like I had told her to. I think she just wanted to make sure I was going to take her side and not offer the belligerent man a drink on the house or something.

"What do you mean get out? I was given the wrong drink and now I'm somehow in the wrong for complaining?" the man shouts.

"You were given the wrong drink, but it was replaced with the right one. And if you want to make a complaint, you ask for me or the manager and you calmly explain why you are unhappy. You do not get to scream in my staff's faces." I say. "Now I will say it one more time before I call the police and have you arrested for harassment. Get out."

The man gives me an angry look, but he turns around and storms towards the door.

"Fucking dick," I hear him muttering as he walks.

I wait until he gets to the door and then I can't resist shouting after him.

"Have a nice day sir," I shout.

This gets a laugh from everyone in the bar and a slammed door from the man as he leaves. I beckon Tania back to the bar once I'm sure the man isn't coming back.

"Can you hop on serving while I go and see if Rebecca is ok, please," I say. "One of us will be out to help you with the glasses in a minute."

"Sure," Tania says, coming around the bar and ducking underneath the countertop.

I smile at her and then I go along to the break room. Rebecca is sitting at the table, but she jumps up when I enter the room. She still looks pretty scared. I hate that. I hate men who yell at women and scare them like this, especially over something that wasn't even an issue.

"Are you ok?" I ask Rebecca.

She nods her head but as she does, she bursts into tears. I feel so bad for her. I would always feel bad for any member of staff who got yelled at by a customer to the point that it upset them, but this is even worse because Rebecca has so much going on with her treatments for her breast cancer. If anyone can do without this, it's her.

"I'm sorry," Rebecca says, sniffling. "I'm just a bit emotional today and then that guy yelling at me on top of that, it was all just a little bit too much."

"It's ok," I tell her. "You don't have anything you need to say sorry for."

I go to her and pull her into a hug. She wraps her arms around me. After a few seconds, I try to move away but she keeps ahold of me, so I hug her for a moment longer. It's starting to become uncomfortable, and I try to pull away again. This time when she doesn't let me go, I drop my arms to my sides. Rebecca keeps hold of me for a second too long even after I drop my arms away from her and I'm getting really uncomfortable by the time she releases me.

"Sorry," she says again when she finally does let me go.

"It's ok," I say. "None of what happened out there was your fault. The customer has been asked to leave and he won't be welcome back here again."

"You defended me?" Rebecca says.

"Well sure," I reply, shocked that she even has to ask.

"I knew this moment would come," Rebecca says, her sniffling turning into a smile.

"What moment?" I ask.

I have no idea what she's talking about. Has this man yelled at her before and no one thought to tell me?

"This moment. The moment you come around and realize you loved me all along," she says. "You defended my honor because you finally see that you and I are meant to be together."

"No, I," start, but Rebecca doesn't stop and let me get a word in.

"You know that Friday I wanted off to go to the hospital?" she says.

Her abrupt change of topic throws me so much that I just mutely nod.

"I didn't really go to the hospital. There a huge bridal fair upstate and I had to go. I just had to. I was so scared you would find out and I would be in trouble but now you feel the same way as I do so it's ok for you to know. You're hardly going to be pissed off that I've got my dress for our wedding are you," she says.

There is so much to unpack here that I just don't know where to start.

"I'm sorry I had to lie to you," Rebecca goes on. "But you were so sweet when you thought I was ill and I didn't want to lose that tenderness between us, so I kept it going."

"Wait," I say. "Are you telling me you don't really have cancer? You just made that up?"

Rebecca nods her head, beaming like it's something she's proud of.

"Yes, exactly," she says. "So, you don't have to worry about taking advantage of me when I'm ill and vulnerable or any of that."

"So, all the treatments you're supposed to have been getting, they were all lies," I say.

"Lie is a nasty word. They were... necessary inventions," Rebecca says.

"Who the fuck lies about something like that Rebecca," I say.

I'm really struggling to keep my temper here and I try

my best to do so because I'm sure I must have missed something along the way. Surely Rebecca hasn't fully lied about this.

"Someone who will do anything for love. Don't you think it's kind of romantic? I just had to get the dress of my dreams because I knew one day you would come around to us and when that day came, I didn't want to not be able to find my dream dress," Rebecca says. "My original plan was just to say the tests came back clear. And then... well you were so nice to me when you thought I was ill... I couldn't bear to give that up."

She's talking like this is normal, like she's a little bit sheepish that she skipped out on work but that's it. She doesn't seem to understand that lying about having cancer is sick. I'm too shocked to speak. I still don't know how to even begin to unpack this. I try to put the cancer lie to one side, and even then, the whole thing is massively fucked up. Who buys a wedding dress to wear at a wedding to someone they aren't even dating?

"Say something Gabe," Rebecca says, but I don't. I can't. I have no words. "Ok. Actions speak louder than words, right? Isn't that the saying?"

I nod because bizarrely, she seems to be waiting for me to confirm that she is right about this being a saying. She smiles at me and before I know what's happening, her lips are pressed against mine and her arms are snaking around my waist.

I pull my head back and turn it to the side when she chases it. I put my hands around my back and gently lift Rebecca's hands off me.

"Rebecca, this is too much," I say. "All of it. The lies. The kissing. The cancer."

"No, don't speak like that," Rebecca says. "I promise it

won't be like that now. I just had to do whatever it took to get my man that's all. I would never lie to you now that we're together."

"Well, you failed because you don't have me. We are not together, and we never will be. I am with Clarissa, and I love her dearly. I'm sorry Rebecca. I have put up with a lot of shit from you. Like a lot of shit. But no more. We're done here. You're fired. Please get your things together and leave the premises.

"But..." Rebecca starts, and I shake my head.

"Wait... I..." she tries again, and I shake my head again.

It's my only response to anything she says now, and she soon gets pissed off and storms off to gather her things and go.

31

GABE

Because of firing Rebecca, I ended up having to work the bar myself until the end of the night because it didn't seem fair to leave Tania to deal with it on her own. It wasn't her fault what had happened. I also had to update Penny and apologize for leaving her rosters messed up.

I'm finally home. I expect Clarissa to be already in bed but when I go into the living room, she's in there reading by the light of a small desk lamp beside the couch. She puts her book down as I come in.

"Where the hell have you been? I've been worried sick," she says.

"What? I was at work. I realize I'm late and I probably should have called you but if you were worried, you could have called me," I say.

"I did. About fifteen times," Clarissa says. "It just kept going to voicemail."

I pull my cell phone out and look at it and see my battery is completely dead and my cell phone is off.

"Fuck," I say. "My battery is dead."

I go to the bedroom and find my charger and come back to the living room. I plug my cell phone in and sit down beside Clarissa.

"I'm sorry," I say. "I didn't mean to worry you."

Clarissa sighs and then shrugs.

"It's ok," she says. "But please, next time, call me if you're going to be late, ok?"

"I will," I say.

"So, I guess the bar was busy then?" Clarissa says.

"No more than usual," I tell her. "But we were down a member of staff. You'll be pleased to know I fired Rebecca."

Clarissa turns in her seat so she's facing me as I sit beside her. She has one leg bent at the knee on the cushion in front of her.

"Why? What happened?" she asks.

"It's absolutely crazy," I say. "And you're probably not going to believe me."

"Oh, I'll believe you. Rebecca is bat shit crazy so anything she's said or done is unlikely to surprise me," Clarissa says. "But it must be bad for you to fire her while she's in the middle of her chemo."

"Well, that's all part of it. Her having breast cancer and having to go for treatments? It was all a lie," I say.

"No way. Who told you that?" Clarissa says.

Judging by her reaction, Rebecca has indeed managed to surprise her.

"She did. A customer was yelling at her and I threw him out. I went to see if Rebecca was ok, and she was crying. I gave her a hug and then she started saying that she knew I'd come around and feel the same way as her and all this," I say.

"I knew she had a thing for you still," Clarissa says.

"Well yeah. You were right. She pretended she'd found a

lump in her breast so I would definitely give her the day off she needed. But she didn't need it to go to the doctors or the hospital or anything. No, that would be too normal. Instead, she went to a bridal show so she could get the dress of her dreams and bought a wedding dress. For our wedding," I tell Clarissa.

She looks at me in open-mouthed astonishment and then she actually laughs.

"Wow. I mean I knew she was crazy but even I didn't think she'd go that far. I did try to warn you though, didn't I?" she says.

"Yeah. You did and I should have listened. I'm sorry. Anyway, after that little confession, I was reeling and so I asked her the first thing that came into my mind which is why she kept on pretending she was going for treatments. She said her plan had been to say everything came back negative but because I was nice to her when I thought she had cancer, she decided to keep the ruse up until I fell in love with her," I say. "And then to top it all off, she fucking kissed me. That's when I found my voice and fired her."

"Can you fire someone for kissing you?" Clarissa asks.

"Well sure if it's an unwanted kiss, it could be classified as sexual harassment. But I'm not worried about that. If she tries to sue or anything, I'm sure I'm justified for sacking someone who has been getting extra, paid days off every week because she's supposedly getting treatment for cancer," I say.

Clarissa considers this for a moment and then she nods.

"Yeah, you're likely right. Gabe, can I ask you something?" she says. I nod and she pauses for a moment. "Is there any part of you that feels anything for Rebecca?"

"Are you shitting me?" I ask. "What, you think I didn't

like her when she was normal but now, she's gone loco I'm going to fall for her?"

"No," Clarissa says. "Of course not. "I didn't mean if you just fell for her today. I meant have you ever had feelings for her? Or have you two ever dated or anything like that?"

"No, honestly no to both," I tell her. "I'll admit at first, I used to flirt a bit with her. I thought it was a bit of harmless fun, but then I saw that maybe it was more than that for her and so I stopped it, not wanting to lead her on."

"And there's definitely nothing between you now?" Clarissa says.

"No. Definitely not," I say. "Where is this coming from Clarissa?"

"I... I don't really know. It's just well, I know Rebecca is crazy and everything, but it makes me wonder. Like the way she hated me from the start because I was close to you and the way she was so sure you would come around to being with her that she bought a freaking wedding dress. It feels like maybe you were together once and split up but that you still have feelings for each other or whatever," she says.

We're meant to be taking things slow but fuck slow. I always promised myself I would tell Clarissa how I feel about her when the time feels right. And this is it. This is the time that feels right. I lean towards Clarissa and take one of her hands in both of mine.

"Clarissa, listen to me. Nothing has ever happened between Rebecca and me and nothing ever will. I have never had feelings for her. I have never liked her. I mean I can see she's attractive, but I've never felt attracted to her. Do you know why?" I ask. Clarissa shakes her head and I look her straight in the eye and hold her gaze. "Because she's not you."

Clarissa's cheeks redden slightly, and she smiles but she doesn't look one hundred percent convinced and so I go on.

"Don't get me wrong, I've had relationships. But my heart has never been fully in them, because I have never found anyone who compared to you. And now we're together, do you really think I'd do anything to fuck that up?" I ask her. She shrugs her shoulders and I laugh softly. "Trust me. I wouldn't. I've waited fifteen years for this."

I stop talking and Clarissa keeps looking into my eyes, searching my face for the truth. I keep quiet for a moment and let her find it. She smiles and I think she's there, but I need to say it. I need her to hear the words directly from my mouth.

"Clarissa, I have loved you for as long as I can remember. And being with you only makes me love you more and more. What I'm trying to say is I am completely, madly a thousand percent in love with you," I say.

She smiles again. She looks down at our clasped hands and then she looks back up at me.

"I love you too," she says. "All the world and back again."

I take her face in my hands and kiss her. She has just made me the happiest man in the whole world.

Our kiss is long and deep and loving, and I never want it to end, but inevitably, it does end. Clarissa pulls back slightly, taking her mouth from mine. She stands up and holds out her hand to me. I take her hand and she leads me out of the living room towards the bedroom. She is practically running by the time we reach the bedroom door. She pushes the door open and looks over her shoulder at me with a soft laugh.

"We are so, so bad at taking things slowly," she says.

32

CLARISSA

My shift this afternoon has gone by in a blur. I didn't think it was possible to be this happy, but here I am, proof that it is indeed possible. I feel like I'm walking on air – fuck I feel like I'm dancing on air let alone walking on it - and I know that my happiness is visible because a few people have commented on how different I seem at work today.

I still can't believe yesterday went from me thinking there might be something between Gabe and Rebecca to him telling me that he's in love with me. When I asked him if he had any feelings for Rebecca or if anything had ever happened between them, of course I was hoping he would say no. But never in my wildest dreams did I allow myself to hope that he might not only say no to having feelings for Rebecca but also confess his love for me.

And then of course there's the other thing. I did a pregnancy test yesterday morning as planned, and I had fully planned to talk to Gabe about it when he got home after work yesterday. But then he was late and then we ended up talking about crazy Rebecca. After that, he told me he loved me, and I knew I had to have him. I took him to the bedroom, and we made love. I planned on telling him once we got our breath back, but he'd had a long day and he fell asleep before I got the chance to talk to him about it. I debated waking him up, but I figured one more day wouldn't hurt. And I held back from talking to him about it this morning because I had to rush off to work for lunch time and I wanted us to have plenty of time to talk when I finally did get to tell him.

Now that we've told each other we love each other, any nerves I had about Gabe's reaction to me being pregnant with his child have dissipated and I can hardly wait to tell him he's going to be a daddy.

My shift is over now, and I say my goodbyes to the other bartenders and then I leave the building. It's only seven pm – it's still light and I feel perfectly safe walking home at this time, but I don't have to. Gabe's car is waiting for me as I leave the bar, the engine idling as it sits at the curb side. I go and get in the car.

"How was work?" Gabe asks me as he pulls away.

"Good," I smile. "It was fairly quiet but the people that were in were all decent people, and it went by pretty quickly. How was your day?"

"Not bad. I missed you," he replies.

"I missed you too," I say with a smile.

We reach the apartment building and go inside and up to the apartment.

"I'll start on dinner while you get changed out of your work clothes if you like," Gabe says once we're inside.

"Actually, there was something I wanted to talk to you about first," I say.

"Ok," Gabe says. "Let's go and sit down."

We go through to the living room and sit down side by

side on the couch. I smile at Gabe and then I reach out and take one of his hands in mine.

"So," I say. "I have some news. You're going to be a daddy."

"Huh?" Gabe says, looking confused. I wait a moment and his confusion turns to a big beaming smile. "Wait. You mean you're pregnant again?"

"Yeah," I say.

Gabe pulls me into his arms, and we hold each other. We're both laughing and crying at the same time and then we're kissing each other, our lips salty with tears. Finally, we pull apart and Gabe puts his hand lightly on my belly.

"Hi there little one," he whispers.

He kisses me again and then he pulls back.

"Right. Screw cooking. I'm taking you out to eat," he says. "Let's celebrate."

"Sounds good to me," I say.

"Is the Marlow Grill ok or do you want to go out of town?" Gabe asks.

"The Marlow Grill sounds great," I say, getting to my feet. "I'll go and get changed."

33

CLARISSA

W e've had a lovely meal. I had vegetable soup followed by a delicious creamy chicken pasta and then a slice of honeycomb cheesecake. Gabe had the soup as well and then he had lamb chops with minted mashed potatoes followed by a chocolate fudge brownie. Both were fantastic and the place has a lovely atmosphere too.

It's just dark enough to feel private while still being light enough to see your food. Soft music plays in the background and candles flicker on each table. The restaurant is just busy enough to have a bit of an atmosphere without being so busy that it makes the place too noisy or the service too slow.

I sip my coffee and smile at Gabe.

"So do you want a girl or a boy. And don't give me that I'm not bothered as long as it's healthy shit. You must have a preference," I say.

"I kind of want a girl because they're usually all about their dads. But then I think when she's a teenager how scary it'll be to let her go off into the world and I think maybe I would prefer a boy," Gabe says. "What about you? Boy or girl?"

"I don't mind," I say.

"Oh no," Gabe says with a laugh. "I wasn't allowed to take the easy route out so neither are you."

"I'm not," I say, laughing with him. "I genuinely don't mind because I want us to have at least two of each. I don't care what order they come in."

"Four children?" Gabe says.

I nod and smile at him.

"Yeah. At least. Is that alright?" I ask.

"It's perfect," Gabe replies. He smiles at me. "Have you thought about names?"

"Yes of course. I'm thinking of Jasmine Lily for a girl or Sebastian James for a boy," I say.

"Well, there's one more reason to hope for a girl then," Gabe says.

He laughs, his eyes twinkling with amusement when I give him a shocked look.

"You don't like Sebastian?" I ask.

"Only for crabs," he says, still laughing.

"Ok then. What name do you like?" I say, determined to hate them.

"Strangely I liked Lily for a girl, but I could live with it being a middle name and her being called Jasmine. For a boy I like Jake or George."

I wrinkle my nose.

"Not George. We had a dog called George when I was a kid. Don't you remember that?" I ask.

"Well, I do now," Gabe laughs. "Ok. Not George. So, Jake then."

"I don't know. I'm not a huge fan to be honest. You're right. We should just have a girl," I say.

"Well, we have plenty of time to think about it," Gabe says. "But the more I think about it, the more I think I do want a girl."

"Our little Jasmine Lily," I smile, lightly rubbing my hand across my tummy.

Gabe puts his hand on top of my other hand where it rests on the table.

"Whatever we get, I can't wait to be a father," he says. "I don't know if I'll be any good at it, but I intend to try to do my best by you and our baby every single day."

"I think you'll make a great father," I say. "You're sweet and gentle and you always look for the good in people. I think those are all great qualities for a parent."

"Ah we'll see," Gabe says. "Luckily if I do turn out to be shit at being a parent, our baby is going to have the best mommy in the world so we're all good."

"Oh God don't be so sure about that," I say. "I'll mostly be winging it."

"I don't believe that for a second," Gabe says. "But even if it were true, I think everything would turn out just fine in the end either way, because with us for parents, one thing our baby is never going to be short of is love and I think that's the most important thing anyone can give to a child."

I squeeze Gabe's hand. That's the sweetest thing that he's just said, and I think it is also very true. Our child will never feel unloved, that's for sure. He squeezes my hand back and for a moment, we just smile at each other, looking into each other's eyes. I have never felt more in love or more loved than I do at that moment. I never want the moment to end, but of course it has to at some point, just not yet.

I don't know how long we've sat just gazing at each other and reveling in our love when there is a cough from beside our table. We look up and see our waiter standing there. He puts our bill on the table between us.

"I'm sorry," he says. "I don't mean to rush you, but we've been closed for ten minutes."

As he says it, it kind of hits me that the tables around us have the chairs stacked on top of them and that I can smell cleaning products in the air. Gabe and I have been so wrapped up in each other, I hadn't noticed any of this happening and I can only assume he didn't notice either. There's no way he would have forced the waiter to approach us this way if he had seen they were closing.

"Oh my God. I'm so sorry," I say, feeling my cheeks burning.

"It's ok," the waiter says quickly but I shake my head.

"No. It's not ok. I'm a bartender and I know how annoying it is when people overstay their welcome," I tell him. "It's no excuse but we are celebrating, and we just lost track of the time."

Gabe has signed the check and left a pile of cash on the table.

"Thank you," he says. "And sorry for us overstaying our welcome. I hope the tip makes up for it."

"Wow. Thank you," the waiter says as he picks up the cash.

He walks away from the table as Gabe and I stand up and get our jackets on.

"How much did you give him?" I ask.

"One hundred dollars," Gabe said. "Like you told him, we know how annoying it is when people don't leave at closing time."

We head out of the restaurant. Our waiter and the hostess follow us out and lock the door.

"Sorry again," Gabe says to them.

The waiter waves off our apology.

"It happens, honestly it's fine," he says. "You were nice about it, that's the main thing. You'd be surprised how often it happens and when it does, how often the people who have overstayed are rude to us for pointing it out."

We say good night and start towards home. Gabe didn't bother bringing the car as the restaurant is only a few minutes' walk from home. We clear the restaurant front and then we pass the thrift shop I saw the first night I moved back here and still haven't gotten around to visiting. As we reach the Indian restaurant, its shutters are down. I notice a set of concrete stairs leading below ground level at the restaurant.

"What's down there?" I ask Gabe.

"It belongs to the restaurant," he says. "It's their cellar and storerooms as far as I know."

I peer over the black railings. The stairs end in a small concrete square. It's surrounded by brick with a shuttered door opposite it and nothing else. We're almost walking by the gate that leads to the stairs when a car screeches to a halt beside us. The driver's door slams open and what looks like a crazy person jumps out.

It's a woman, I can see that much. Her long hair is straggly and wild and sticking up all over. Her top has a small hole in it just about where her belly button should be. She isn't wearing any shoes. In her hand, she's holding a knife with a long, sharp looking silver blade. I feel my mouth go dry at the sight of the blade. Gabe seems to notice it at the same time as I do because he takes a half step forward so that I'm behind him.

The deranged woman comes closer to us, and she happens to step into a pool of light being left by a street-lamp. I gasp when I recognize her face. It's Rebecca. Her eyes are wild, practically rolling in their sockets and her lipstick is smeared up one cheek, but I still recognize her.

"Rebecca?" I say quietly. "What's happened? Are you ok?"

"No, I'm not ok you man stealing whore," Rebecca shouts.

She shouts so loudly that I'm waiting for lights to start popping on in the apartments above the shops. They don't come on, but I hear footsteps coming closer behind me and I glance back and see the waiter and the hostess from Marlow's Grill approaching. They're coming up slowly, assessing the situation clearly able to see that something isn't right here.

"I didn't steal anyone," I snap.

"Oh really?" Rebecca screeches. "Gabe and I were well on our way to getting together when you came back to town. Fucking bitch."

"No, we weren't Rebecca," Gabe says softly. Then he turns his attention to me. "Come on. Let's go."

"What? You can't even bear to give me two minutes of your time, is that it?" Rebecca demands.

"Not while you're waving a knife around and acting like a crazy person, no," Gabe says.

Rebecca rolls her eyes and drops the knife on the ground beside her feet. I feel a whole lot better that she's no longer waving it around, punctuating her words with it.

"There. Now can I have a minute of your time?" she says.

"What exactly is it that you want?" Gabe asks her.

"Well, I suppose the short answer to that question is that all I ever wanted was you, Gabe. I didn't think it was too much to ask really. I'm a nice person and I don't think I'm bad looking. But I get it. You don't want me like that. I'm just wanting to let you know that I've made my peace with that," she says.

"Ok. Well, that's good. I'm glad to hear it," Gabe says. "And I never meant to make you think you were bad looking or not a nice person."

Rebecca smiles at him but it's not a nice smile. It's a cold smile, like the ones she used to give me at work, the ones that made me feel shaky inside.

"But here's the thing Gabe. I've accepted I can't have you," Rebecca says. "But I will never accept that she can."

She looks at me in disgust when she says it and then before I know what's happening, she runs at me and slams her hands against my shoulders. The impact sends me reeling and I fly backwards. My ass and lower back hit the railing behind me, except they must hit the gate part because they don't stop me; they don't even slow me down. I keep stumbling backwards, trying to keep my footing when suddenly I take a step there is nothing but air beneath my foot and I'm falling.

"If I can't have him, no one can," I hear Rebecca shouting as my back connects with the hard, sharp edges of the concrete stairs.

I cry out as pain slams through my body, but I'm not done yet. I roll down the stairs, head over heels, head over heels, slamming my body off the stairs, the walls, everything. By the time I reach the bottom of the stairs, I'm unconscious.

GABE

For a horrible moment I can't move. I'm frozen to the spot while everything around me moves in slow motion showing me every horrible detail in bright, vibrant colors that make me feel sick to my stomach.

Rebecca smiles at me. Well, if you can call it a smile. It's more like a snarl, an animal expression where Rebecca shows me her teeth without any sort of humor or warmth in her eyes. It's at that moment that I realize she's not harmless crazy, she's downright dangerous crazy.

"But here's the thing Gabe. I've accepted I can't have you," Rebecca says. Her voice is loud and devoid of any emotion except perhaps anger. "But I will never accept that she can."

When Rebecca says 'she', she looks straight at Clarissa and the expression on her face is as though she's standing in something disgusting. I open my mouth to tell Rebecca to fuck off but before I can, she charges from where she's standing and runs towards Clarissa. She raises her hands and they connect with Clarissa's shoulders.

Clarissa goes flying through the air. I want to reach out

to her, but I can't move. I want to shout something, anything, but I can't speak. She hits off the railings around the stairs and I almost breathe a sigh of relief but then I see she's still falling backwards. She hasn't hit the solid fence; she's hit the gate and now she's through it and she's still moving backwards.

One more step and her arms pinwheel wildly and then she's gone from my line of sight.

"If I can't have him, no one can," Rebecca shouts.

I ignore her. Fuck her and her ridiculous ideas. I don't care about her, I only care about Clarissa. I hear her scream and I assume it's as she hits the stairs. I hear her continuing to tumble and then there's a loud thud which I take is her hitting the ground and then nothing. Silence. The silence is way scarier than hearing Clarissa scream. If she can scream, she's alive.

That thought finally frees me from my paralysis and it seems that at the same time, the waiter and the hostess from the restaurant are also flung into action. The waiter runs at Rebecca and grabs her, pinning her arms to her sides. She tries to get free but he's a lot bigger and stronger than her and her struggles are in vain.

The hostess is on her cell phone. I hear her ask for the police and an ambulance and then I'm moving. I run towards the stairs but as I reach the top, I slow down, terrified of what I might see. I force myself to move forwards, one step at a time, until I can see the bottom of the stairs.

Clarissa is laying on the ground. She's not moving. I start down the stairs taking them two at a time in my rush to get to her. I reach the bottom of the stairs and throw myself on the ground beside Clarissa.

She isn't moving and her eyes are closed but I can see her chest rising and falling as she breathes, and relief fills me. She's not dead. She's not in a good way though. Aside from being unconscious, she has a gash on her forehead that's bleeding, and her left leg is bent at the knee at an angle that no leg should ever be at.

I want to scoop her up in my arms and hold her. I reach out for her but a voice from above stops me.

"Don't," the voice shouts.

I look up and see the hostess from the restaurant on her way down the stairs.

"Don't move her. If she's hurt her back or her neck, you could make it worse," she says. "The ambulance is on its way and the police are too. Joe has the crazy woman and he won't let her go."

I realize the woman is right and so I settle for holding Clarissa's hand.

"Wake up. Please wake up." I say.

The hostess kneels down on the other side of Clarissa.

"I'm Lisa by the way," she says as she feels Clarissa's neck for a pulse. She nods, satisfied that she's found one.

"Gabe," I say.

"Is she your wife?" Lisa asks.

I know she's only asking me questions to take my mind off the situation but despite knowing her plan, it's actually working in that it's stopping me losing my mind completely.

"Yes," I say. "Do you think she'll be ok?"

Lisa nods her head.

"Yes," she says. "Of course."

Suddenly the baby comes into my head, and I feel like screaming. There's no way such a new pregnancy could withstand a fall like that.

"My baby is dead," I whisper.

"She's not dead. She's breathing," Lisa says.

"No, not Clarissa. She's pregnant," I say. "The irony is we

were out for a meal this evening to celebrate the news. She only told me a couple of hours ago. And now our baby is gone, isn't she?" I can't help thinking of her as she. Our little Jasmine Lily. "She couldn't survive a fall like that could she?"

"I honestly don't know," Lisa says. "I mean I doubt it to be honest but try to stay positive until you know for sure."

I nod, but I can't let myself hope and then find out that our baby is gone.

I hear sirens in the distance. They are quickly getting closer, and Lisa gives me a relieved smile.

"Here comes the ambulance and the police," she says.

The sirens get louder and louder until they are right on top of us and then they cut off.

"Down there," I hear the waiter say and then I hear feet running towards us.

Hands touch me and I try to shrug them off. I see Lisa getting to her feet opposite me and I realize the hands are the paramedic. He's trying to move me so that he can get to Clarissa. I also realize that he's speaking to me, explaining who he is and what he's doing. I jump up and get out of his way.

"Sorry," I say.

"It's ok," he replies.

The paramedics work together to get Clarissa onto a backboard. They put a collar on her neck and then get her onto a stretcher which they pick up and go back up the stairs. Lisa and I follow. We're about halfway up when I hear more sirens and by the time we reach the top and the paramedics are loading Clarissa into the back of the ambulance, the police have arrived and two of them are arresting Rebecca while a third talks to the waiter from the restaurant.

I follow the paramedics. One of them turns to me.

"We're going to do her vital signs and some preliminary assessments. The police will probably want a word with you. Don't worry, we won't leave without telling you," he says.

I want to argue and demand he let me into the ambulance now, but I know that will do no good. I'll only be in the way, and I would much rather them do what they can for Clarissa here. The police officer who was talking to the waiter comes towards me.

"I'm Sergeant Wallace," he says. "I believe the injured lady is your wife?"

"Yes," I say. "I'm Gabe. Gabe Kerrey. And my wife is Clarissa."

I don't know why I say this. It just feels like something he should know, and it wouldn't be something the waiter could tell him.

"We've gotten a witness statement from the gentleman out of the restaurant," Sergeant Wallace says. "We will need to speak to you and get your statement too, but first I'm sure you want to go to the hospital with your wife. If you can come to the police station tomorrow and give your statement that would be great."

I nod.

"Yes. Yes, of course I will," I say.

There would have been a time that I would have begged the policeman not to charge Rebecca. I would have reasoned that she is mentally ill, and she needs help not punishment. Not anymore though. I hope they throw the book at her for what she's done.

"Thank you, Mr. Kerrey," Sergeant Wallace says.

I nod an acknowledgement. Lisa catches my eye as the officer moves towards her and I follow the officer. I pull Lisa into a hug which she returns.

"Thank you," I say. "For calling for the police and the ambulance and stopping me from moving Clarissa."

"Sure," Lisa says. "I hope her, and your baby are ok."

"Me too," I say.

"YOU CAN GO IN NOW Mr. Kerrey," the nurse says to me as she leaves Clarissa's room.

I feel like I've been sitting in this corridor forever. No one has told me anything about Clarissa. I start to ask the nurse if she is ok, but I decide that it will be easier to ask Clarissa herself. She must be conscious now or they wouldn't be letting me in.

I thank the nurse and go into the room. Clarissa is sitting up in bed in the center of it on a load of pillows, a sheet draped over her just below her breasts. Her arms are crossed on top of the sheets. She turns her head when she hears me come in and she smiles, her face lighting up when she sees it's me and not another doctor or nurse.

"You're awake," I say needlessly. "How are you feeling?"

"Sore," Clarissa laughs.

She lifts the sheet up at the side and shows me her leg in a cast. The cut on her head has been cleaned and stitched up.

"My back hurts too but the doctors have said it's just bruised," she says.

"And the baby?" I say, barely daring to ask.

"Is perfectly fine," Clarissa beams. "She's a strong little thing."

"Just like her momma," I say as I pull Clarissa into my arms.

We hold each other for so long that I start to get a cramp

in my leg the way I'm standing. I don't care though. I don't make any effort to move away from Clarissa. She is more than worth a muscle cramp.

"I love you so much," Clarissa says.

"I love you too," I say. I lightly touch her stomach. "And you little one."

We kiss and I feel like I've died and gone to heaven. I'm with the woman of my dreams and we have been given a second chance with the life growing inside of her. And I won't waste that chance. I will do whatever it takes to keep both Clarissa and our daughter safe and happy for the rest of my life.

The End

EPILOGUE

CLARISSA

One Year Later

The trial is finally over. It's been a long two weeks waiting from the day I gave my testimony until the sentencing, but the thing is finally done. Rebecca has been sentenced to a minimum of five years in a secure psychiatric hospital. Gabe was a bit upset that she didn't get sent to prison, but I'm glad she's going to get the help she so clearly needs. I think in the year waiting for the trial to come around, I mentally forgave Rebecca.

She clearly had a lot of mental health issues and my leg healed and there was no lasting damage. And while I wouldn't go all psycho killer like Rebecca did, I can only imagine how I would feel if Gabe loved someone else instead of me. So yeah. I get it.

"Are you nearly ready? We're going to be late unless we leave in the next two minutes," Gabe says, coming into our bedroom.

He stops when he sees me.

"Wow. You look stunning," he says.

"Thank you," I smile. "And yes, I am almost ready. I just need to find my other earring."

I'm wearing a cream-colored dress with red flowers on it and a slit up one side. I have one of the ruby earrings I want to wear in my hand, and I've lost the other one. Gabe laughs and I frown.

"What's funny?" I ask.

"You are," he replies, crossing the room and kissing my cheek. "Your earring is in your ear."

I reach up to my ears and feel the missing earring is indeed in my ear. I laugh and shake my head and then I put the other one in.

"Right, let's go," I say. "Where's Jasmine?"

"All ready to go sitting in her car seat," Gabe says.

"And Penny, Sav and Matt all know where to meet us?" I ask.

"Yup," Gabe says. "Now will you relax. Jasmine Lily's christening is meant to be a happy occasion not a reason to panic. Of course, her godparents know where to find us."

"Ok, yes, you're right. I'm sorry. I'm going to stop stressing out now," I say. "I'm just going to enjoy the day."

And really, what's not to enjoy? I'm about to spend the day with the man of my dreams and all of our friends and family while we officially welcome our gorgeous daughter to the world.

The End

COMING NEXT - SAMPLE CHAPTERS

TAMING THE CEO BEAST

Prologue

Axel

My eyes felt grainy as I pulled into the rest stop. A quick check of my watch showed I'd been driving for thirteen hours nonstop and hadn't slept for thirty-two hours straight. Had it not been for the fact my body felt as though it was going to give up the ghost, I probably wouldn't have stopped. But I didn't want to end up in a ditch somewhere, or under an eighteen-wheeler so my family would have the task of planning a double funeral. How ironic it would be! I could see the headlines:

Son killed in accident on his way to father's funeral. More news at ten.

I sighed and rubbed my hands over my face as I sat in the parking lot for a few minutes. I was just over two hours from home. It still felt surreal. My thoughts went back to the morning last week when my sergeant told me I had a phone call.

The last thing I had expected to hear was Axel Vance Sr. had left the land of the living.

The last conversation I'd had with my father a month ago was still ringing in my ear. He was brimming with health. Of course, he grumbled his company wasn't doing as well as he wanted, but his personal investments were doing extremely well, and he seemed happy to be taking off to the Mediterranean with a group of friends. Afterwards, he had a Safari expedition in Africa lined up. I winced when I remembered joking that if he even put ten percent of the energy he spent on vacations into his company it wouldn't be struggling the way it was.

Well, that company was mine now.

I frowned. It had never crossed my mind that I would be expected to take over Vance Security Solutions so soon. In fact, I had an assignment overseas in a few weeks and would be away for a few months. Hopefully, I could talk his vice president into running operations until I returned.

I got out of the truck and stretched, acutely feeling every sore muscle in my six foot three frame. I was tough, but I guess I was human, after all. I checked to ensure that my weapon was concealed beneath my uniform, then entered the diner. I found an empty table in a corner where I had a view of the dining room and my back against the wall. I scanned the menu just as the waiter approached.

"Evening, soldier. What'll it be?"

"Coffee. Is your BLT any good?"

The lanky man grinned. "You better believe it. Folks come just for the BLT."

"In that case, make it two. One to go."

"Sure thing."

A minute later, I took a sip from the steaming mug in my hand and looked around the room. A young couple was to my right. The man stared with adoring eyes at the flushed cheeks of the animated woman next to him, while she excitedly held her hand out in front of her and wriggled her fingers, to let her ring catch the light.

I guess, she said yes.

I turned my gaze over to the other table. A family of three. Their girl, she must have been twelve or thirteen was chattering happily while her parents looked on indulgently. I saw the flash of her dimples as she smiled up her mother. Her father smoothed her flaxen ponytail and patted her on the head, before he bent to whisper something in her ear. She burst out laughing at the private joke and I averted my gaze, as my thoughts returned to my own father.

An older couple stood to leave. The woman walked with a slight limp and the man held a steadying hand beneath her elbow. I watched as he assisted her through the door.

The three couples could have easily represented the stages in relationships. But where did I, a twenty-two-year-old soldier, fall in the picture?

The girl laughed and my eyes went back to the family. From the snippets I could hear, she had been spending a few weeks with her grandparents and her parents had picked her up a few hours ago. I remembered a time when I was like her. Excited about being with my grandparents, or even my parents, for that matter.

I took another sip of coffee as I watched the young girl. She was so innocent, as all children are. I wondered when she would be thrust into the harsh realities of the world. How long could her parents shield her from the atrocities of this world?

I had seen so many already. In my naivety I had chosen the military because I thought I could help me to save the world. I would be the sheep dog protecting my flock from the wolves. If I had my way, no one would ever know pain, sickness, or hurt. Girls like her would be untouched. They would all find their sweethearts as the woman with the ring and live happily ever after. But I knew better now.

All I could do now was hope her parents protected her for as long as they could. The object of my contemplation turned suddenly and caught me staring at her. With a big grin on her lips she raised her hand to her temple and saluted. I touched my temple briefly with my fingers and turned away.

My sandwich came and my stomach rumbled as I dug into it. The waiter was right. It was good. But then again, cardboard would have tasted like heaven now. I hadn't eaten for close to twenty-four hours as I had done double duty for a few days in order to have these few days off for the funeral.

Of all the things to take him out, a common cold. A cold which quickly progressed to pneumonia. And it was over before anyone could process what was happening. The few times I had spoken with my mother since his passing she had sounded as though she was still in a fog. Understandably so, but distressing.

My parents had been the anomaly of arranged rich marriages: they had actually loved each other. In fact, they were childhood sweethearts. They had been devastated to learn that I was to be an only child as another pregnancy was risky for my mother. So I had the love of ten children poured on me. My eyes clouded briefly as I realized in a few hours, I would face the task of putting him into a hole in the ground forever.

Suddenly, I felt the hair on the back of my neck stand. My gun was pressing against my flesh as I glanced around cautiously.

I looked beyond the waiter who was approaching my

table and felt a cold hand grip me as I looked in the direction of the door.

A disheveled man with wild eyes had pushed his way inside. The instant I saw him dip into his waist, I knew what was happening. I reached for my gun and shrank back into the wall, knowing my uniform made me stick out like a sore thumb.

"Nobody move! You move, I shoot your fucking head off!"

He grabbed the waiter by the collar and hauled him to the register.

"Gimme all the money! Now!"

I could hear the shrieks as the other workers ducked for cover and see the woman behind he counter shaking as she emptied the contents of the register into the bag the robber was carrying. I sat quietly, calculating how long it would take me to cross the floor and disarm him. But the way he was looking around with jerky, strange movements told me he was probably as high as a kite. And being that high with a weapon equaled a dynamite with it's pin already pulled. Besides, just my uniform would make him react badly.

He grabbed the bag with the money and I waited for him to leave. But instead, he began to look around the dining room. The instant he saw me, I knew I would have to discharge my weapon. The only problem was the girl and her parents were between us.

Everything seemed to happen in slow motion. He raised the gun and pointed it at me. I heard screams as the mother covered her daughter's face. The scream seemed to break his concentration and I saw him turn to look at the couple. I was halfway out of my seat when he pounced forward and grabbed the girl. The mother instinctively lunged for him and I heard a single shot ring out. The woman slid to the ground, blood already beginning to pool underneath her.

I heard the girl scream as the father stood, shock etched on his face, and began to move towards the shooter.

"Come anywhere near me and I'll kill her too," he screamed, as he swung his gun and caught the side of the father's face. His victim crumpled to the ground.

The robber dragged the kicking screaming girl to the door, brandishing the gun the whole time. The second he was outside, chaos erupted in the diner. The staff knelt over the unconscious mand and bleeding woman. I could hear the workers calling the paramedics. I was already out of my seat and heading out the door into the warm summer night. My training kicked in as I covered the few feet in record speed. They'd not gotten far, and the little hostage was not going quietly.

I could see he had her by the hair as she continued to fight. As he raised his hand to hit her, I tackled him. The girl fell one way and he fell another. He had been so focused on the girl he had not heard my approach and I caught him off guard. By the time he raised the gun, my fist was already on its way towards his wrist. The blow was so hard he cried out as the gun fell from his hand.

I moved quickly and with a few punches, had him in a daze. I looked up at approaching footsteps and saw some of the workers.

"I need rope!"

"Got some."

One of the waiters helped me to tie the guy's hands behind him. I turned to the girl who was shaking like a leaf. I knelt by her and put my hands on her head to feel her scalp. She winced, probably from where he had tugged her hair. I smoothed her hair away from her face. In the light of the lamp post in the parking lot, her clear hazel eyes looked back at me. The warmth and innocence I had seen in the diner just a few minutes ago, were now replaced by terrible fear.

Her skin was clammy. She was going into shock. I rubbed my hands along her cheeks and her arms.

"What's your name, sweetheart?"

"L-Lisa."

"You're safe now, Lisa."

I stood swung her into my arms. Her little hands clung to my shoulders as I strode across the parking lot. Before I could step inside, a frantic waitress burst outside.

"Don't bring her in here!"

"I want my mom and dad," the girl begged. Her bottom lip trembled as her eyes filled with tears. I looked at the waitress. She was looking at the girl with a pitiful expression. Then she looked at me. And I knew.

"Don't bring her in here," the waitress whispered, again tears clogging her throat.

I felt a dead weight in my arms and looked down. Lisa had fainted.

A crowd had begun to gather outside and we could hear the wail of the ambulance in the distance. I looked down at the girl in my arms, wishing with all my heart that I could have protected her a little longer from the harsh realities of this cruel world. In a split second, life as she knew it had changed forever.

I sat on the tail of my truck as I looked at the scene unfolding before me. The paramedics had arrived a few minutes ago. I had handed Lisa to them. They immediately placed her into the vehicle and closed the door. I watched as the police taped off the scene and began processing the robber. He was now conscious and sitting in the back of a police car. I had already given my statement but for some reason I could not move.

My gut tightened into a knot as the stretcher came out, a sheet covering Lisa's mother. I swallowed hard as bitterness rose within me. For a few dollars, a woman's life had been taken. A husband was without his wife. A daughter without her mother. I stared at the stretcher as it rolled to a second vehicle. Life was so unfair.

"Vance?"

I looked up at the police officer who spoke.

"Thanks for being here and what you did. The situation could have been far worse and we would have a double homicide on our hands."

I shook his hand.

As the parking lot emptied, I got into my truck and pulled out onto the highway. I had to go bury my father.

***

Chapter 1
Lisa

Ten Years later

"Lisa? Honey?"

"Coming, Dad!"

I attached one more bead in the series so that I would not lose track of my work when I came back. I hurried into my father's room. He was half standing, half-leaning against the four-poster bed. His cane was a few feet away out of his reach.

"Dad! Why didn't you call me sooner?"

"I thought I could get to it."

I shook my head at him and pursed my lips in mock severity.

"Are you trying to get me fired from my job as cane-getter and general caretaker?"

He laughed and swayed unsteadily. I picked up the cane and placed it in his hand. I masked my concern with a smile as his fingers trembled with the effort to hold the cane steadily.

"Do you have it?" I asked gently, my hand on his back.

He nodded silently. But I could see his jawline was tight as he gritted his teeth with the effort it took for him to take even a few steps. It seemed as though every week he became more and more frail. He had another doctor's appointment tomorrow. But I could almost hear the conversation already.

We will need to run some more tests... he is a healthy man... all his vitals are reading well... it's a mystery. Why is a forty-eight year old healthy man declining so rapidly?... we will need to run some more tests... we need to keep him overnight for observation...

Usually by the last suggestion my father would put his foot down. He was adamantly against any sort of hospital-ization. He had likened it to having one foot in the grave and had declared that the day he set foot in a hospital was the day he had decided to join my mother.

The first time he had said it a few years ago after his first doctor's visit, I had felt a cold claw grip my insides. It had been shortly after my eighteenth birthday, but six years had still not dulled the heartache of what had happened that night in the diner.

I remember waking up in the ambulance while the para-medic was checking me over. Gone was the bright blue gaze of the soldier with a crescent scar at the corner of his left eye. In its place was a dark-haired woman with equally dark eyes, prodding and poking me. Through the back window I had seen blue lights flashing. Then suddenly, the back door opened.

"Keep her here," a gruff voice had announced before slamming the door shut once more.

I remember the kind gaze of the paramedic as she smiled at me. It had not quite reached her eyes, eyes that had been filled with pity as she looked at me. It had been a day later that it had all made sense. My mother's body had been loaded into a separate vehicle, my father by her side.

"I'm sorry, Lisa. I shouldn't have said that," he apologized afterwards.

I looked around now to find my father standing at my elbow, his back bent slightly and his weight on the cane. I could only hope that tomorrow's appointment yielded something substantial. I didn't want him to be among the statistics as a rare condition that had been diagnosed when it was too late.

I placed my hand under his elbow as he took a few steps across the room. We stopped in the doorway to allow him to rest. Today seemed to be worse than yesterday. He needed the cane more these past days.

He smiled at me and his face lit up. He was still a very handsome man despite the physical challenges he was having. As a matter of fact, there was nothing wrong with his mind and heart. It was just his legs and hands that were the problem.

I helped him into the living room with some effort, and he took a seat in his favorite armchair by the window. Though it was summer, I placed a light blanket across his knees and handed him one of his magazines. I bent down to place the water bottle within reach and kissed his cheek gently.

"If you need me, I'll be right over there."

I pointed exaggeratedly at the table where all my beads were spread out.

I resumed my task of making a set of waist beads for a bridal party. The client would be picking them up this evening. But I was through before midday and had them all packaged and ready to go.

This was the pattern of my days and had been for the past two years when my father became sick.

At first, he had ignored the weakness in his limbs and attributed it to fatigue. But one morning when he had fallen in the shower and couldn't get up, I had gotten the neighbor to assist me. I had taken the day off from my new job as a secretary. By the end of the month, I had been released as I had either been taking more days off or coming in late while tending to my father. After the fall, he had taken a disability leave. Thus began the series of doctor visits, hospital tests, various diagnoses, and the depletion of any emergency savings we may have had.

After a year, my father's job had given him the option of taking early retirement for medical reasons with a portion of his pension. And I had become his main caregiver. Many twenty-two year olds would have stuck their parent in a home and moved on with their lives. But all we had was each other. And that was how it had been for the past ten years.

He had rearranged his life for me, ensuring I lacked no time or attention as I went through my awkward teenage years. The period of life when a girl needed her mother most, he was there, filling the gap the best way he knew how. So now the tables had turned and it was my time to be there for him.

It had taken strategic management and systematic

saving to keep our heads above water financially. My mother had a few investments which we had refused to touch unless absolutely necessary. I had skipped college and had done a one-year certificate secretarial course as I had not wanted to go to college at the time. I was thankful I didn't have a student loan hanging over my head at a time like this. With his illness, I worked either part-time or from home. I had signed up with an employment agency and got a few temporary jobs through them. I had also picked up a hobby of jewelry making and found that I was not half bad. I had a few clients and advertised by word of mouth. The bridal set was through a friend of a friend. Every penny counted, no matter how small.

That evening after the order had been collected and paid for, I sat at the dining table. I had seen to it that dad was comfortable in bed, the remote control and tablet close at hand. I pulled out my laptop and opened the excel file with the data for the monthly expenses. One by one, I added up every cent I had earned from jewelry and the few days I had gotten a transcription job. Then I added my father's pension and the monthly allowances he received from his insurance policy. Then I began deducting the bills: rent, utilities, medication, food. I looked at the figures and breathed a sigh of relief. The bead job had allowed us to break even this month and I didn't have to dip into our savings. Dad's medication was still partially covered by insurance. Had it not been for that insurance coverage, we would have been in the poorhouse a long time ago.

I closed the laptop and got ready for bed. The last thing I did before I showered was check the windows and door. One could never tell with a ground floor apartment. After my shower, I checked on my father. The room was dark as he had turned off the television. But I could see his face in the light of the tablet.

"Hey, Dad."

He looked up at me and smiled.

"Hey."

"I'm heading to bed now. Rest well, okay?"

"You too, sweetheart."

"I love you."

"I love you too."

I looked at him a little longer before I moved away from the door. I stood in the shadows where he couldn't see me. I heard him sigh deeply.

"Irene, you would be so proud of her. She's got a heart of gold. We raised her well. I miss you so much, baby. Rest well in heaven."

I felt as if a fist was squeezing my heart. Irene. My mother.

Quietly I slipped away from the door and went to my room. I lay staring into the darkness for a long time before sleep came.

Over the next few weeks, our pattern continued. More tests. More possible diagnoses. More experimental treatment. And we were both weary of it all. And to make matters worse, I could feel as though my father's fighting spirit was growing weak. I could feel him giving up the war for his health. And if that happened, he was as good as dead. And I knew why he was giving up. In a few days, we would relive that awful night. This year would make it ten. We both missed my mother terribly, but I knew he missed her more. It was my fear that if whatever he had did not kill him, a broken heart would.

The day before the anniversary of mom's death, I went grocery shopping. I deliberately chose that day and uncharacteristically went to get the groceries rather than have them delivered as usual. The neighbor from upstairs was watching Dad while I went out. She was a sweet woman and former nurse, so I was confident he was in good hands.

I stopped at a flower stand on the corner and made a quick purchase before I hopped on a bus. The ride was a short one. But it could have lasted for eternity for all I cared. It was a ride I never wanted to take each year, but forced myself to take for my father's sake. Tomorrow he will take the ride with me. I had budgeted for a cab as he would not be able to handle the walk to and from the bus stop. My stop came up too quickly and I disembarked.

I stared up at the wrought iron sign, my eyes clouding with tears. I clutched the bouquet as I walked quickly among the headstones. I found the spot, shaded by a tall oak tree. I brushed away the leaves that had covered the ground and pulled the weeds that had grown up since the gardeners had last weeded. I traced her name on the headstone. Irene Evadne Mulligan.

I sat at the foot of the grave and looked at the headstone.

"Hi, Mom. It's me. Lisa. Well, it has to be me, right? I'm the only child you had. Unless you've gotten others that I don't know about in heaven. Am I a big sister to some little angels?'"

I laughed at my own joke. Then my throat clogged with tears.

"Dad isn't doing well, Mom. He misses you terribly. We both do. But I know he misses you more. There isn't a day that goes by that he doesn't talk about coming to be with you. He tries to joke about it, but I know he's serious. He blames himself for that night you know. He keeps saying it should have been him and not you who tried to rescue me. He keeps saying I should have been sitting beside him. He keeps saying that you should have lived and he be the one taken. Oh, Mom! I blame myself too! I just had to stop and use the restroom. And then I just had to get something to eat. Why did I make us stop? You would be here right now if it wasn't for me!"

Sobs ripped through me as I poured out my heart to my mother. When the worst of the storm had passed and the gulping sobs became soft whimpers, I stood and wiped my face. I looked at the headstone for a few minutes more. I kissed the bouquet and placed it in the center.

"I love you, Mom. Dad and I will come tomorrow. But I had to see you first. I will continue to be brave. And I will continue to fight for him. I will continue to be strong."

I knelt once more and touched the headstone. Then without a backward glance, I walked out of the cemetery.

I got the shopping done before stopping in at the craft store. I usually had my orders delivered, but took advantage of browsing in person as only so many things were in the online shopping portal. I bought a few items, using my discount card and the sales discounts for a further discount.

By the time I got home that afternoon, my spirits were lighter. Dad was sleeping. I slipped a ten into the neighbor's hand as she left. I got started on a simple dinner of chicken with mashed potatoes and beans that could be kept warm until we were ready to eat. Then I buried my nose in my bead tray. I had no orders, but I liked to keep busy. Sometimes I posted pictures of my work on social media and had an instant sale. At the back of my mind I knew I needed to find a real job.

I was halfway through the necklace when Dad woke up. I went to assist him to the bathroom then to the living room. Apart from his afternoon naps and bedtime, I tried to keep him out of bed. I did not want him to become an invalid and bedridden.

He sat at the table as I dished up the meal.

"I'm thinking of getting a job, Dad."

"Oh!" He frowned. "What about your jewelry business."

I smiled confidently. "Well, that can be part-time until it grows a bit more."

He smiled, even thought his face looked sad. "It'll grow. You'll see. You're a good designer and your time will come."

We ate in silence, after that.

While he watched television, I tidied the kitchen. I could tell his thoughts were nowhere near the comedy on the screen. We both were miles away. But we'd get through. We always did.

That night after I put him to bed, I went through my nightly routine of locking up and showering. When I slipped into his room to say goodnight, I was surprised to find that he was already asleep. That night as I lay staring at the ceiling, I wondered how he would hold up tomorrow. Not only that, I wondered if I would have him by my side next year, or if he would get his wish and be by my mother's side instead.

The only thing I knew I could do was get a job that would keep us both sheltered, clothed, and fed. The rest was out of my control.

*****

Chapter 2
Axel

I strode through the airport, feeling eyes on me as I did. My sunglasses hid my expression as I walked by. I knew the image I presented. Who would not look twice at a tall, well-built man with a buzz cut and a thick black beard? Especially if you were a woman. There was power in every step. I exude masculinity and knew it. I also knew my confidence rolled off me in waves. And people just felt safer with me nearby. That was the intention. I was a walking brand. It also helped that the polo shirt I wore bore the name and logo of Vance Security Solutions. I'd lost count of the number of casual conversations I had struck up in the terminals I had been in and out of on this trip, and the number of business cards I had handed out with our company information.

Nine years ago, when I had come back home to take the reins of the company my father had left behind, it had felt like I was trying to climb a never-ending mountain. It had taken me months to wade through the mess he had left behind. I had to fire some and hire others. There had been times when it seemed as though we were going to sink. I'd had to rebuild our brand and reputation from the ground up. And now VSS was synonymous with safety and confidence in the products we offered. And if things continued on this trajectory, it could become a global brand. I was certainly working towards that end.

I found my gate for my last connecting flight and waited for boarding. As I watched the planes come and go, I used the rare moment of idle time to reflect on the last decade.

Losing my father had been a blow. Somehow children never expect their parents to die. Worse if they were in the prime of their life and the death was rather sudden. The overseas duties right after his funeral had come at a good time as well. I had needed the space to deal with myself. I knew my mother loved me and meant well, but the last thing I needed then was her hovering over me. Our separation after the funeral had done us both a world of good. When I had returned, we had both begun our healing process. I couldn't say we were entirely okay even after ten years as grief never ends. But we were much better with the passing of time.

I watched as my plane taxied up to the boarding gate. I had my boarding pass in hand and my backpack. I had been out of the country for a month, refreshing my combat skills as well as renewing my international licenses as a security service provider. In all the years of traveling I had done, there was never any greater feeling than that of returning home. It had only been in the last year or two, though, that I had felt confident in being away from the company for longer than a few days. I had a good staff for the most part. I knew I was a hard taskmaster. Those who could deal with it, stayed. Those who couldn't, left. For the past year, I had noticed a trend of those leaving, though. After my father's assistant, who I had inherited, retired last year, I couldn't seem to keep an assistant. I didn't know what it was. But they didn't last more than a few weeks.

Before I had gone on my trip, I had dismissed Nadine. She had been, what, number ten? Admittedly she had lasted the longest – an entire month. But just when I thought I would finally have someone who I could depend on, she had left without a backward glance. I hated to think it had anything to do with my exacting instructions regarding the way I wanted the suits in my closet to be arranged. And so, what if I had gotten into a shouting match with her regarding a document she had misfiled, only to find it where she had said it would be? And so what if that shouting match had been in the middle of the entire office and I had continued to yell at her, despite the file being found? She had called me every name under the sun and I had told her if she hated working with an asshole of a pig such as I was (her words, not mine), she could leave. She had taken my advice and done just that. The last thing I had done before leaving for my trip was to contact the temp agency and put in my request for an assistant. Each time I called them, I always waited for them to tell me they were unable to fulfill my request. But they never did. And so, Monday morning I met Geraldine. She lasted a week.

A few months after my return, I raced through assistants once more. It was beginning to wear on my nerves and I was beginning to lose count. This last one seemed set to break Nadine's record, though. But that was more on my part of not wanting to admit defeat in not keeping an assistant than on her being efficient. As a matter of fact, she was one of the most inefficient ones yet. And I was reaching my boiling point. Her dismissal was inevitable. Yet still, I would give her enough rope with which she could hang herself. As I waited in my office one Friday evening, I felt as though her hanging day had come.

I was furious. I could feel the blood coursing through my veins, growing hotter with each passing second. Where the hell was that dimwit of an assistant?

I turned smartly on my heels as I made another circuit of my office. I knew that everyone was on edge as they watched me through the open blinds. Good. I wanted them to be on edge. That was the only way to run a tight ship in this operation.

I checked my watch once more. Only Elizabeth Vance could think of throwing a party at this time of the evening, peak hour and a Friday at that, and expect every guest to be in attendance. Her excuse was that her bedtime was eleven and she would be damned if she would inconvenience herself for the sake of those who could not make it at her five pm start time. If ever I wanted to know where I got my sense of entitlement in having things done my way or else from, I didn't have to look further than my mother. But being her only child didn't exempt me from her wrath. I was supposed to be at my mother's half an hour ago. A whole fucking thirty minutes late already, not counting getting dressed and the one hour drive it would take for me to get there in rush hour traffic. Something had told me some shit like this was going to go down when I saw time passing and no sign of Deidre, my nincompoop of an assistant. The transportation contingency, the helicopter, was waiting on the roof even as I paced. The journey would be ten minutes at most.

I looked up as I heard a buzz of conversation. I saw a flash of red curls. Deidre.

"Out of my way! I'm late! He's going to kill me for sure!"

"Just let us know where you want to be buried."

She stopped, one hand on her hip, the other holding a suit bag over her shoulder.

"Now is not the time for your stiff jokes, Candace."

Candace, one of the marketing agents, stared her down.

"Now is not the time to be arguing with me about my jokes. You're the one that's in hot water." She pointed her chin at my office and I watched as Deidre turned to look at me staring at her.

"Oh shit!"

She moved as though she was on fire and in a few seconds, she was in my office.

"I'm so sorry Mr. Vance, sir. But I have your suit."

With a flourish, she presented the suit bag. She even had the audacity to smile and curtsey. I looked at her coldly.

"Do you have any idea what time it is?" I spoke softly, deadliness coating every word.

"I know you're a little late-"

"A *little* late? Try almost an hour, not counting travel time."

"I'm sorry sir, it's just that-"

I cut her off as I opened the bag and examined the suit. I felt as though my blood pressure was going to go through the roof.

"What is this?" I held the suit out to her.

She moved from one foot to the other uneasily.

"Well, you see-"

"No. I don't see. What – is – *this*?"

"I know I was supposed to pick it up yesterday. But by the time I got to the cleaners they were closed. And they're not open today."

I looked up at the ceiling and closed my eyes. I took a deep breath before I looked at her.

"Would you care to explain to me why a suit that I personally left at the cleaners last week just so that I would not be in a rush to have it cleaned, was not picked up during the full eight hours of their daily operation any time before they closed yesterday? Why?"

"Ummm. I-I forgot."

I blinked a few times. "You *what*!?"

"Forgot. I forgot," she barely whispered.

"Didn't you write it down in your diary?"

"I did."

"And?"

"I left my diary at the office."

"What is the point in having a diary if you're not going to read it?"

"But I got you another suit! I went to your house and picked the best one you have in the closet."

"You picked a gray suit for a black and white event."

"I didn't know!" she began to wail.

"There's a lot you don't know."

"I'm trying my best, sir!"

"You're not trying hard enough."

"I'm going to do better. I promise!"

"See that you do."

I started to take off my shirt and heard her gasp. Right now, I could care less about offending her sensibilities whether to my scars or my muscles. I ripped the shirt off and was in the process of putting on the shirt she had brought when my cell phone rang. I swore softly as I saw my mother's number. I was in deep shit. I put the phone on speaker.

"Yes, Mother?"

"Um, sir. May I go now?"

"Not yet."

"Axel Lionel Vance! I don't believe you! How could you treat your own mother this way?"

"Sorry, I was unavoidably delayed at the office, but I'm taking the helicopter out so I'll be there before you know it."

"I'm not talking about your tardiness. That's another discussion, but do you have any idea how humiliated I feel right *now*?"

"Sorry-"

"And your assistant of all people!"

I stopped in the middle of buttoning my shirt. I stared at Deidre who was staring at the phone as though it was a loaded gun pointed at her.

"What about my assistant?"

"Donna called me *this morning-*"

"Her name is Deidre."

"Donna, Deidre, Diane. Her name could be Dumbo the flying elephant for all I care. She called me this morning in the middle of my spa treatment. I had the phone on speaker Axel! Now the whole city knows that Elizabeth Vance's son does not give two hoots about his mother."

I continued to stare at Deidre. She had gone as white as a sheet and was wringing her hands while doing that hop from one foot to the other which I absolutely hated.

I tried to speak as calmly as possible. "What are you talking about."

"Why didn't you buy my birthday gift before today?"

"What?"

"Your assistant called me in the middle of my spa treatment to ask me what I wanted for my birthday. At first, I thought it was a joke someone was playing on me. But then she said she was *your* assistant and you had told her to get my gift. You couldn't even do it yourself, Axel? I am so *embarrassed*! And even now at the party I can tell that people are whispering about it. 'Didn't you hear? Her own son didn't get her a gift. He's not even here. He had one of his little workers get her something at the last minute. How absolutely *awful* for her!' I know what they're saying behind my back while they smile in my face."

I sighed. "Those were not my instructions to Deidre. Your gift was already bought. She was supposed to pick it up." My eyes narrowed on Deidre who looked as though she was praying for the floor to open up and swallow her up and save her from my wrath. "Unless she forgot to do that too."

"I beg your pardon?"

"Nothing." I saw Deidre began to inch away. "Don't you dare leave now."

"What!?"

"Not you, Mother. I have something to deal with here at the office. There are necks to be squeezed."

Deidre yelped and ran out in a flash. Exasperated, I

watched as she scurried to her desk. She grabbed the appointment book from her messy desk and scampered out before I could call out to leave the appointment book behind she had no more need for it. And I, needed another new assistant, but it would have to wait until Monday morning.

"So, Mother, is this event strictly black tie, or can I wear the gray suit I'm wearing now?"

Please pre-order the book here:
Taming the CEO Beast

ABOUT THE AUTHOR

Thank you so much for reading!
If you have enjoyed the book and would like to leave a
precious review for me, please kindly do so here:

The Forgotten Pact

Please click on the link below to receive info about my latest
releases and giveaways.
NEVER MISS A THING

Or
come and say hello here:

ALSO BY

Nanny Wanted

CEO's Secret Baby

New Boss, Old Enemy

Craving The CEO

Forbidden Touch

Crushing On My Doctor

Reckless Entanglement

Untangle My Heart

Tangled With The CEO

Tempted By The CEO

CEO's Assistant

Trouble With The CEO

It's Only Temporary

Charming The Enemy

Keeping Secrets

On His Terms

CEO Grump

Surprise CEO

The Fire Between Us